Derwent May

Hannah Arendt

Penguin Books

Penguin Books Ltd, Harmondsworth, Middlesex, England
Viking Penguin Inc., 40 West 23rd Street, New York, New York 10010, U.S.A.
Penguin Books Australia Ltd, Ringwood, Victoria, Australia
Penguin Books Canada Ltd, 2801 John Street, Markham, Ontario, Canada L3R 1B4
Penguin Books (N.Z.) Ltd, 182–190 Wairau Road, Auckland 10, New Zealand

Published in Penguin Books 1986

Grateful acknowledgement is made to the following for permission to reprint previously
published material:
The University of Chicago Press for extracts from *The Human Condition* by Hannah
Arendt © 1958 by The University of Chicago. Reprinted by permission.
Martin Secker and Warburg Ltd and Harcourt Brace Jovanovich Inc. for extracts from
The Origins of Totalitarianism © 1951 by Hannah Arendt, renewed 1979 by Mary
McCarthy West. Reprinted by permission.
Jonathan Cape Ltd and Harcourt Brace Jovanovich Inc. for extracts from *Men in Dark
Times* © 1968 by Hannah Arendt. Reprinted by permission. Originally published in
the *New Yorker*.
Faber and Faber Ltd and Viking Penguin Inc. for extracts from *Eichmann in Jerusalem*
© 1963 by Hannah Arendt. Reprinted by permission.

Made and printed in Great Britain by
Richard Clay (The Chaucer Press) Ltd,
Bungay, Suffolk
Filmset in Monophoto Photina by
Northumberland Press Ltd, Gateshead,
Tyne and Wear

PENGUIN

HANNAH ARENDT

Derwent May is a novelist and critic, and the Literary Editor of the *Listener*. His novels include *The Laughter in Djakarta* (1973) and *A Revenger's Comedy* (1979), and he is also the author of *Proust* (1983), a study of *Remembrance of Things Past*.

LIVES OF MODERN WOMEN

General Editor: Emma Tennant

Lives of Modern Women is a series of short biographical portraits by distinguished writers of women whose ideas, struggles and creative talents have made a significant contribution to the way we think and live now.

It is hoped that both the fascination of comparing the aims, ideals, set-backs and achievements of those who confronted and contributed to a world in transition, and the high quality of writing and insight in these biographies, will encourage the reader to delve further into the lives and work of some of this century's most extraordinary and necessary women.

CONTENTS

Hannah in her thirties (Fred Stern, Bildarchiv Preussischer Kultur-besitz)

Hannah with her first husband, Günther Stern, in about 1929 (the Hannah Arendt Estate, courtesy of Lotte Kohler)

Hannah's second husband, Heinrich Blücher, as a young man (the Hannah Arendt Estate, courtesy of Lotte Kohler)

Hannah with Heinrich Blücher in about 1950 (the Hannah Arendt Estate, courtesy of Lotte Kohler)

Hannah in Maine with one of her closest friends, Mary McCarthy (the Hannah Arendt Estate, courtesy of Lotte Kohler)

Hannah lecturing at Chicago University (the Hannah Arendt Estate, courtesy of Lotte Kohler)

Hannah teaching at the New School (the Hannah Arendt Estate, courtesy of Lotte Kohler)

Hannah in her early sixties (Fred Stern, Bildarchiv Preussischer Kulturbesitz)

ACKNOWLEDGEMENTS

I am very grateful to Miss Eva Beerwald, Hannah Arendt's stepsister, for the many hours I spent in her home in Muswell Hill, London, listening to her vivid memories of Hannah as a girl and after the war. I am also most grateful to Miss Mary McCarthy and her husband, Mr James West, for their hospitality in Paris and for the delightful and illuminating picture of Hannah that Miss McCarthy unfolded for me. Other people who gave me memorable personal impressions of her were Mr Daniel Bell, Sir Isaiah Berlin, Miss Paula Deitz, Rabbi Albert Friedlander, Mr David Green, Mr Hans Jonas, Mr Melvin J. Lasky, Mrs Shirley Letwin, Mr Frederick Morgan, Lord Quinton and Mrs Helen Wolff.

No author writing about Hannah Arendt now could fail to owe a deep debt to Elisabeth Young-Bruehl for her massive pioneering biography *Hannah Arendt: For Love of the World*. I have referred in my text to essays on Hannah Arendt by Jurgen Habermas, Hans Jonas, Judith N. Shklar, Sheldon Wolin and Miss Young-Bruehl that appeared in a special commemorative issue of *Social Research* (Spring 1977), the journal of the New School for Social Research in New York, where both Hannah and her husband taught; and I have quoted various articles by Alfred Kazin, Robert Lowell, Mary McCarthy and Sheldon Wolin that appeared in the *New York Review of Books* (13 May 1976, 22 June 1976, 24 June 1982 and 26 October 1978 respectively). I have also referred to three books about the

New York literary scene during and after the war: Lionel Abel's *The Intellectual Follies*, William Barrett's *The Truants* and William Phillips's *A Partisan View*. Remarks I have quoted by W. H. Auden come from *Encounter* (June 1959); by Martin Jay from *Partisan Review* (XLV, No. 3, 1978); and by Uwe Johnson from the *Frankfurter Allgemeine* (December 1975). Mr Philip French kindly provided me with a transcript of a programme about Hannah Arendt that he produced on BBC Radio 3 on 11 February 1980; participants whose contributions I have mentioned are Hans Jonas, Jerome Kohn and Elisabeth Young-Bruehl. The quotations from Theodor Adorno are from his book *Minima Moralia*. Other books and journals referred to are identified in the text.

I should like to thank Miss Lotte Kohler, co-executor with Mary McCarthy of Hannah Arendt's literary estate, for her kind help in providing photographs.

Mr John Dunn, Mr D. J. Enright, Mr P. N. Furbank and my wife, Yolanta, read this book in manuscript, and I am very grateful for their valuable comments.

1906	Hannah Arendt born in Hanover, Germany.
1910	Her parents return with her to their native city, Königsberg.
1913	Hannah's father, Paul, dies of syphilis.
1920	Her mother, Martha, marries again. Hannah goes with her to live in the house of her stepfather, Martin Beerwald.
1924	Goes to Marburg University to study philosophy.
1925	She and her professor, the philosopher Martin Heidegger, become lovers for several months.
1926	Goes to Heidelberg University, and becomes a friend of the philosopher Karl Jaspers.
1929	Marriage to Günther Stern. Publishes her doctoral thesis on St Augustine.
1930–33	Increasing involvement with Jewish opposition to the Nazis.
1932	Starts her first book, the biography *Rahel Varnhagen*.
1933	Leaves Germany for France, after Hitler comes to power.
1933–39	Working for Jewish refugee organizations in Paris.

1936	Günther and Hannah separate. Hannah meets Heinrich Blücher and begins to live with him.
1939	Divorced from Günther Stern. Finishes *Rahel Varnhagen* (but it is not published until 1958). Martha leaves Germany and comes to Paris.
1940	Marriage to Heinrich Blücher.
1941	Hannah, Heinrich and Martha escape to New York.
1941–45	Writing for *Aufbau*, a German émigré paper in New York.
1944	First contribution (on Kafka) to *Partisan Review*. Begins to know a circle of New York writers.
1948	Martha dies.
1951	Becomes famous with the publication of *The Origins of Totalitarianism*.
1958	Her major work, *The Human Condition*, is published.
1961	Attends trial of Adolf Eichmann in Jerusalem as reporter for the *New Yorker*.
1963	Publication of *Eichmann in Jerusalem* in the *New Yorker*, and in book form. Violently criticized by many Jews and loses many friends. Publication of *On Revolution*.
1968	Supports student rebellions in America and France.
1969	Death of Heinrich Blücher.
1970	Publication of *On Violence*.
1973	Gives Gifford Lectures on 'Thinking' at Aberdeen University.
1974	Has heart attack while giving second set of Gifford Lectures, 'Willing'.
1975	Death of Hannah Arendt.
1978	Posthumous publication of *The Life of the Mind*.

ONE

1906–24: Growing Up in Germany

Johanna Arendt was born in Hanover on 14 October 1906. It was a moment of peace and prosperity in Germany. The parents of the young Hannah (as she was always to be called) were members of a generation that had grown up without any personal experience of war. Germany had been united after the Prussian success in the war against France in 1870–1; it had grown powerful under the rule of the Chancellor Bismarck and by 1914 it would be the greatest industrial nation in Europe. The old ruling classes still held on to their power, but there was universal suffrage, there were welfare provisions in advance of any in the world, and the Social Democratic Party, though it had a large Marxist or Communist element, acted as a constitutional political party. Hannah's parents belonged to it, though they held moderate political views.

Both of them, Paul and Martha, came from well-established Jewish families in Königsberg, the provincial capital of East Prussia, a quiet town on the Baltic; and they returned there when Hannah was three. Here she was to stay till, in her teens, she set out determinedly to enjoy a wider world than

Königsberg could offer. There was a university, the Albertina, in Königsberg; but it had lost the lustre it had in the eighteenth century, when the philosopher Immanuel Kant was among its professors. However, his statue stood in the square, and pointed the way for Hannah.

She seems to have been happy as a small child. In 1984, her stepsister, Eva, still recalled Hannah's mother saying: 'Hannah loved cherries when she was little. Every year in February she'd start asking "Are the cherries ripe yet?"'

But there was less happiness in store in the years immediately ahead. The reason for the Arendts' return to Königsberg was that Hannah's father was suffering from syphilis. He had thought himself cured before his marriage (and certainly Hannah was free of congenital syphilis); but its later stages suddenly declared themselves, and he had to give up his job in Hanover, where he had been working for an electrical engineering firm. His health declined rapidly and he was taken into a psychiatric hospital in Königsberg in the summer of 1911. He died there two years later – in the same year as his own father, Max Arendt, who had been like another father to Hannah in the absence of hers. After this year, 1913, when she was seven, those who knew her well could see that Hannah kept a deep sorrow buried inside her.

The Arendts were Jews; but in Königsberg, as elsewhere in Prussia, the majority of educated Jews had assimilated to German life to a greater or lesser degree. They felt themselves to be very different from the poor Jews – the *Ostjuden*, or eastern Jews, as they were often known, though the word lacked accuracy as marking a distinction, since the forebears of many of the prosperous Jews had also originally come from

Russia. In their daily lives, families like the Arendts had very much the same preoccupations as other middle-class Germans, and many of them wholeheartedly shared the interests and passions of German culture and politics.

In her first major work, *The Origins of Totalitarianism*, Hannah Arendt was to write about the strains of assimilation for Jews in nineteenth-century Germany. Jews, she said, were faced with two main options: that of remaining a pariah, excluded from German society, or that of accepting the unattractive role of the parvenu, who must show the qualities of 'inhumanity, greed, insolence, cringing servility, and determination to push ahead' if he 'wants to arrive'. And even if he managed some accommodation to a more ambiguous, in-between role, his situation was not exactly a comfortable one: 'Jews felt simultaneously the pariah's regret at not having become a parvenu and the parvenu's bad conscience at having betrayed his people and exchanged equal rights for personal privileges. One thing was certain: if one wanted to avoid all ambiguities of social existence, one had to resign oneself to the fact that to be a Jew meant to belong either to an overprivileged upper class or to an underprivileged mass which, in Western and Central Europe, one could belong to only through an intellectual and somewhat artificial solidarity.'

This harsh and searching exposition of Jewish difficulties clearly had its aptness for many of the nineteenth-century Jews she was writing about – and was also an expression of a state of mind which Hannah herself, with her fine moral instincts, was later to suffer deeply from. What her own solution was we shall see.

But such stark difficulties were, equally clearly, not the daily lot of most of the Jews Hannah knew in her childhood. She herself later acknowledged that 'the word "Jew" was never mentioned at home ... My mother was not very theoretical ... the "Jewish Question" had no relevance for her.' That was not to say that as a child Hannah did not encounter anti-Semitism: 'All Jewish children encountered anti-Semitism. And the souls of many children were poisoned by it.' But Hannah's mother was brisk and matter-of-fact about the family's Jewishness. 'Of course she was a Jewess! She would never have had me christened, baptized. And she would have given me a real spanking if she had ever had reason to believe that I had denied being Jewish.' She simply instructed Hannah that if any of her teachers made anti-Semitic remarks, the girl was to get up and go home, and leave her mother to write a letter of explanation and complaint. As for remarks by other children, Hannah had to deal with those herself and not speak of them. So at that time, in her own words, 'these things did not really become problematic for me. There existed house rules, so to speak, by which my dignity was protected.'

Nor did Hannah have much contact with Jewish religion. The only time she went to the synagogue was as an act of courtesy when she was paying a visit to one or other of her grandmothers. But of course the 'Jewish Question' was being discussed in Königsberg, as elsewhere. And one figure who was later to become very important in her own relationship to it, a prominent Zionist called Kurt Blumenfeld, was a friend of her grandfather's and played with her in the Arendt house when she was still a baby.

On the outbreak of war in August 1914, the newly widowed Martha fled with Hannah to Berlin, along with thousands of other Königsbergers. The Russian army was advancing and it was feared that Königsberg would fall to it. But the Russians were repulsed, with terrible losses, at the Battle of Tannenberg, and before the end of the year the Arendts were home again. Martha had enough money from her own family to be able to survive, with some help from taking in lodgers. For the rest of the war, life in Königsberg was to continue much as in peacetime.

Hannah was now at school, being taught according to the serene Goethean principles that sought to inculcate the right balance between inner development and a relationship with the outer world. This was a view of life that implied a pre-established harmony in the universe between man and nature, and between man and man. Other people, in this view, were 'the mirror images which reflect the inner self', and which help to make that inner self 'more distinct'. It seems unlikely that Hannah experienced any such feeling of harmony between herself and the world; and before long it was the two German philosophers who most decisively attacked such a world-view who were to become her mentors.

But after a period of ill-health at the beginning of the war, she quickly started responding to her lessons, and her ability began to be noticed. She was growing, too, into a girl with striking looks: thick, dark hair, a long, oval face, and brilliant eyes – 'lonely eyes', a young man, Hans Jonas, saw them as, when he met her at the age of eighteen, but 'starry when she was happy and excited', as Mary McCarthy described them many years later, with 'deep, dark, remote pools of inward-ness'.

In 1920, when she was thirteen, her mother married again. Martha's new husband, Martin Beerwald, was a rather serious, middle-aged Königsberg businessman, also Jewish, whose wife had died a few years before, leaving him with two teenage daughters – Clara, who was now twenty, and Eva who was nineteen. Eva has spoken of the thrilling new life that her stepmother's arrival brought into their quiet, musical household. Suddenly it was full of spirited people, many of them interested in Social Democratic politics, as Martha herself still was; and Eva came to regard Martha as her own mother, or 'Mutt', the person who taught her to understand and enjoy human relationships for the first time.

But to her mother's regret, Hannah never entered with any enthusiasm into the life of the new family. Perhaps she could never regard it as her own. The gang of three girls was not a very satisfactory one – Eva and Hannah were always joining up in opposition to Clara, or Clara and Hannah were joining up against Eva. Nevertheless, they did many things together, like holidaying at the seaside, where Hannah went night-fishing with the Baltic fishermen. There is a photograph of Hannah and Eva dressed up for a fancy-dress party in 1922, when Hannah was sixteen. Eva is wearing the cap and short trousers of the boy in the Swiss folksong who goes begging with his marmoset (she actually has a guinea-pig in the box she is holding); Hannah is dressed up as some kind of symbolic cigarette-girl, with a high, cylindrical, cigarette-shaped hat. '*Ach*, she must have been smoking already,' Eva said to me, ironically and affectionately, looking at the photograph, 62 years later. And indeed the fancy dress, for all its fun, must have been intended as a provocation, a sign that Hannah was by now going her own way (she was always, afterwards, a great smoker, of cigars and pipes as well as cigarettes). She turned her room at the Beerwald house into a little salon of her own, where she brought her friends, and formed a 'Greek circle', who read the classics together in the style of German university students of that time.

It was at about this period that Hannah started writing poems. They were usually short lyrics, trying to catch in a few words and an off-hand rhythm some deep, often confused emotion – poems firmly in the German romantic tradition, skilfully written but not profoundly original. However, some of them still seem to speak in a line or two of the adolescent Hannah; there is one in particular, written when she was seventeen:

> *'Was ich geliebt*
> *Kann ich nicht fassen,*
> *Was mich umgibt*
> *Kann ich nicht lassen.'*

> (What I have loved
> I cannot take hold of,
> What stands around me
> I cannot leave.)

Perhaps there we find expressed both her bewildered love for her mother and her home, and her guilty longing to be elsewhere.

If she and her friends wanted to penetrate a more interesting world, however, for most of them it was not, in the early 1920s, the world of politics. After the war, Germany had banished its Kaiser and reconstituted itself as a republic – known as the Weimar Republic, after the town of Goethe and Schiller where the constitution was drawn up. Martha Arendt had not supported the left wing of the Social Democrats, who had now joined the Communists in a group known as the Spartacists; but when the Spartacists led an uprising of the workers in 1919, she took her daughter along to a meeting of her political friends, in great excitement, and told her that this was an historic moment. But the government, which was predominantly composed of moderate Social Democrats, rode the storm, and two of the Spartacist leaders, Rosa Luxemburg and Karl Liebknecht, were murdered. Germany was struggling to maintain itself as a parliamentary democracy; but few of the warring politicians were held in much respect by the people, and many were bitterly hated by one part or other of the nation. The savage cartoons that George Grosz drew of Weimar politicians and businessmen show the radicals' contempt for them, a contempt which many young people, not necessarily radical themselves, shared. In later years, Hannah remarked: 'George Grosz's cartoons seemed to us not satires but realistic reportage: we knew those types; they were all around us. Should we mount the barricades for *that?'*

Politics were to loom larger before many years had passed. But what excited Hannah and her more thoughtful friends at this time were reports they were getting of two philosophers now teaching in German universities: Karl Jaspers in Heidelberg, and a younger man, Martin Heidegger, in Marburg.

What attracted the young to these teachers was, in the first place, the fact that they were not mere interpreters of an accepted, tranquillizing philosophy of the universe – such as were to be found in plenty in the German universities then. Jaspers and Heidegger were clearly original thinkers, who wanted to connect philosophy again with the hard, genuine problems facing anyone who tries to understand the true nature of his existence in the world. Above all, these two men were uncomfortable thinkers, who offered those who listened to them no assurance that they had any guaranteed place in the universe. In 1946, Hannah Arendt wrote a retrospective article about them in the New York journal, *Partisan Review*, called 'What is *Existenz* Philosophy?' That was the name that had come to be given to the line of German thought to which these two philosophers belonged: as Arendt said there, the 'existentialism' associated with Jean-Paul Sartre was a French literary movement of the previous decade, whereas *Existenz* philosophy had a hundred-year-old history. The main source of many of its notions was the nineteenth-century Danish thinker, Søren Kierkegaard, with his concept of *Angst*, or 'dread', as the inescapable response of men faced with the uncertainty of God's existence; but Arendt held that Jaspers and Heidegger had 'reached a consciousness as yet unsurpassed' of what was 'really at stake in modern philosophy'.

Drawing on her own words in that article, we can say that *Existenz* philosophy places man in the middle of a world where he can no longer rely on anything: where nothing universal exists, only the individual. It opposes to all earlier ideas of the universe as an intelligible whole, the forlorn, solitary person who can only be certain of one thing, his existence. It sees all the ancient questions of philosophy, like the nature of freedom, as problems that have no objective answer, but can only be grasped by each individual in his own way. It is the first absolutely and uncompromisingly this-world philosophy, insisting that man's Being is 'Being-in-the-world' – a fearful state, a state in fact of 'not-being-at-home', but one that nevertheless makes the task of 'maintaining oneself in the world' all the more challenging.

These were alluring ideas for Hannah and many of her generation – and the very melancholy that such ideas were supposed quite properly to induce must have found a response in her. So in the autumn of 1924, having passed her *Abitur* or final school examination, and with some financial help from her father's family, she went to Marburg to become a pupil of Martin Heidegger. And there, in the lecture-rooms, she fell in love with him, and he with her.

TWO

1924–33: From Solitude to Politics

Martin Heidegger was thirty-five when Hannah met him; he was married with two young sons. He was himself the son of a sexton in a Roman Catholic church in Masskirch, in the Black Forest, and had been brought up a Catholic though by the time Hannah knew him he was one no longer. He was an exceptionally brilliant man but, in his professional and private life, a cautious one, with small, searching eyes that were often remarked on. He was also, it would seem, rather vain and self-conscious: he was short, and always insisted on sitting down when he was photographed, so that this would be less apparent.

When Hannah joined his classes, he was working out the ideas found in his major work, *Sein und Zeit* (*Being and Time*), which was to be published in 1927. Students sometimes found him impossible to follow, but the best of them felt that in listening and talking to him they were learning to think – and not dead thoughts, but 'passionate thinking, in which thinking and aliveness become one', in Hannah's own words about him.

He responded to Hannah's youth, her beauty and her mind.

Many years later he declared to her that it was she who had inspired his thought in these years of the mid-1920s, which had been his most 'stimulating, composed, eventful period'. They were lovers for several months; he wrote her many letters and poems, and they would meet in the attic room where she lodged. One of Hannah's own poems of this time was about her joyous, forbidden love that would not 'wither the priest's hands'. But the impossibility of keeping up this secret relationship soon became clear to them both; and there was never any question of his giving up his position or leaving his family.

In the summer of 1925, after they had broken off, Hannah wrote a description of herself for Heidegger, which she called *Die Schatten* ('The Shadows'). It was both an exploration of what her love-affair had meant to her, and a tribute to him. It speaks of herself in the third person, and is extremely abstract in conception – yet it contrives to be very eloquent and moving about all that she had felt. After her happy childhood, she says that she had become dull and self-preoccupied for a long time, noticing things but not responding to them with any feeling, and finding a protection for herself in this state of mind. Heidegger had released her from this spell, so that the world had become full of colour and fascination and mystery for her again. But now all her fear had returned, without the habitual estrangement which had guarded her; and this anguish was a far worse spell to live under. Would she ever escape from it?

It is a sad testament; yet, in the light of events, I think it can be said that the love-affair's lasting consequence was indeed to open her afresh to life, if not immediately and not easily. Heidegger was to disappoint her again, perhaps even more profoundly, when he associated himself with the Nazis; yet she never ceased to feel devotion for him. Many of her later utterances about love must have referred to this time. A sentence of St Augustine's that is also very aptly Heideggerian in its phrasing became a favourite remark of hers: 'Love means: I want you to *be*.' And a brief passage about love in her book *The Human Condition* (otherwise not much concerned with the subject) seems also to draw on the revelation that came from her love of Heidegger: 'Love, although it is one of the rarest occurrences in human lives, possesses an unequalled power of self-revelation and an unequalled clarity for the disclosure of *who*, precisely because it is unconcerned to the point of total unworldliness with *what* the loved person may be, with his qualities and shortcomings no less than with his achievements, failings and transgressions ... Love, by its very nature, is unworldly, and it is for this reason that it is not only apolitical but anti-political, perhaps the most powerful of all anti-political human forces.'

Hannah Arendt's own important writing was not destined to be, until the very end of her life, philosophy of the kind she had learned from Heidegger. Yet his influence is very clear in her work. His return to the Greek philosophers, his wrestling with the very etymology of their words to get back to their first, fresh apprehension of the wonder and terror of Being, finds its counterpart in her attempts to base a new, invigorating view of politics on a re-creation of ancient Greek thought in distinctly existentialist terms. And the underlying mood of astonishment at the very fact of existence that runs throughout Heidegger's writing seems to coalesce with Hannah's personal reawakening through knowing and loving him, and to find an echo in the original, challenging way in which she came to look at every question.

She left Marburg at the end of that academic year, feeling that it was impossible to go on living there. After a term in Freiburg, she settled down again as a student in Heidelberg. In her first student year she had been preoccupied with her lover, but now, in the lively atmosphere of this ancient university city, she started making a wider circle of friends. One friend, who had also moved from Marburg to Heidelberg, was Hans Jonas, who has written about her 'genius for friendship' – which in his case, as in that of many other friends she made in Germany, lasted till she died. Jonas has also recalled how they first met 'in Bultmann's New Testament seminar, where we were the only two Jews'. Rudolf Bultmann was a theologian in Marburg, and a typical story attaches to Hannah's presence at his classes: in the style her mother had taught her, she told him, when she applied for permission to attend, that 'there must be no anti-Semitic remarks'. Bultmann promised her gently that if any anti-Semitic remarks should be made, 'we two together will handle the situation'. It must have been moments like this that prompted Jonas to recall that, from those first days, he sensed in her 'an absolute determination to be herself, with the toughness to carry it through in the face of great vulnerability'.

Hannah found other lovers, too, at Heidelberg: a writer from Berlin, Erwin Loewenson, and a young scholar, Benno von Wiese. When Eva, by now a dental technician building up her own business, visited her in Heidelberg for a holiday in the summer of 1928, she found Hannah very happy, in spite of the fact that she had just been thrown out of her lodgings for ruining the curtains with cigarette smoke. Eva recalls that – again – they ate cherries, and Hannah ate hers so rapidly that she had finished a pound of them while the rest of the group had hardly begun. In some photographs of this time, Mary McCarthy particularly noticed Hannah's feet, which already had the attributes this American novelist so admired in later years – 'charming ankles, elegant feet ... [that] expressed quickness, decision. You only had to see her on a lecture stage to be struck by those feet, calves and ankles that seemed to keep pace with her thought' as she moved about.

But probably the most important person that Hannah came to know in Heidelberg was the other master of *Existenz* philosophy, Karl Jaspers, who was her professor there. Jaspers was six years older than Heidegger, but had been much influenced by the younger man. He had begun his career in neuropathology, at the Heidelberg psychiatric hospital, and had only come later to philosophy. For Hannah, he was soon a fatherly presence; and he, like Heidegger, was keen to test out his thinking on clever students like her in the course of working on his own major book, his *Philosophy*, which was to be published in 1932.

He shared with Heidegger the fundamental 'existentialist' convictions; but there was a different tone in his teaching and writing. Heidegger wanted to bring men back to a full, authentic awareness of their Being, in this universe that did not need to be; but his outlook remained sombre. He saw modern technology as rendering men mindless and

27

mechanical, utterly alienated from all sense of their Being, as it incorporated them into its own mindless systems (and here he was nodding across an ideological gulf to Karl Marx and a new generation of German Marxists, who had a similar fear for modern man but proffered a quite different, wholly political explanation and solution). Beyond that, his thought was permeated with the idea of death, the final nothingness that all men must meet, whether or not they face the challenge of the nothingness into which they are born.

Jaspers approached this plight of man with more optimism and good cheer. Hannah Arendt never considered him so profound or determined a thinker as Heidegger: but temperamentally she was soon at ease with him. Jaspers always seemed to express himself as not merely undaunted, but positively excited, by the freedom given to man by finding himself in an empty universe. The fact that there was no authority, no ultimate truth, provided men with the adventure of finding their own truth – and the further adventure of reaching out to other men to share their thought and discoveries. 'Think for yourself, but in your thinking place yourself also in the situation of every other man,' he taught his students. There was a generosity and sympathetic imagination in Jaspers, a thriving sense of men's possibilities if they thought and argued together, that was lacking in Heidegger. We can see his influence behind such splendid later remarks of Hannah Arendt's as this, in an essay she wrote about a Jewish Catholic, Waldemar Gurian, in 1955: 'In the battle of ideas, in the nakedness of confrontation, men soar freely above their conditions and protections in an ecstasy of sovereignty, not defending but confirming with absolutely no defences *who* they are.' She talked and argued with many scholars and students in Jaspers's house, and perhaps first felt that 'ecstasy of sovereignty' there.

Under Jaspers's supervision, Hannah worked on her doctoral dissertation, which she had decided would be a study of the idea of love in the thought of St Augustine. She finished this and published it, as *Die Liebesbegriff bei Augustin* (*The Concept of Love in Augustine*) in 1929, when she was still only twenty-three. It is an austere, systematic study, relating Augustine's different concepts of love to the human experience of time. The greatest value of this work to her was probably the deeper acquaintance it gave her with early Christian thought about virtue and the political life, which helped her more sharply to define her own ideas in due course in *The Human Condition*.

In 1929 she also married for the first time. The man she married was another highly intelligent young German Jew, Günther Stern – a kindly man, the son of two progressive child psychologists who were well known in Germany. Hannah had been acquainted with him in Marburg in 1925, and they met again in Berlin in January 1929 at a fancy-dress ball, where she was dressed – in her usual provocative way – as an Arab harem girl. Hannah and Günther lived together in Berlin for several months – he helped with the final revision of her doctoral thesis – and they were married in September. Hannah's mother liked her new son-in-law, and very much hoped the couple would have children; but the marriage was destined to last only a few years.

Soon after their marriage, the couple went to live in Frankfurt, where Stern wanted to submit a thesis for his

Habilitation, the qualification required for becoming a university lecturer. This was Hannah's first contact with a group of Marxist thinkers with whom she was often associated by critics in later years, but with whom, certainly at first, she had very little in common. This group was based on the recently founded Institute for Social Research, and was to become known as the 'Frankfurt School'. Names of members who later became famous include Max Horkheimer, Theodor Adorno and Herbert Marcuse, and the literary critic Walter Benjamin. Their main preoccupation was to produce a Marxist-based analysis of the effects of capitalist economic relations on culture and thought. They all saw bourgeois capitalist society as enforcing different kinds of rigid mental tyranny on both employers and workers, and thought that a Marxist society would give freer range to the flexibility and imagination of the human mind. In this respect, twentieth-century society caused them to feel a dissatisfaction that – as has been mentioned already – had many points in common with that of the existentialists. Politically, however, the Frankfurt group regarded Heidegger and his followers as naive and dangerous: naive in their failure to recognize the social and economic causes of this 'alienation' of men's minds; and dangerous in so far as their ideas could merge too easily with Fascist worship of the hero and superman.

Later, when most of the Frankfurt group, like Hannah Arendt herself, found themselves in America, the convergence of the ideas of these two sets of German thinkers became more pronounced, especially as the 'Frankfurt' thinkers turned against Soviet Communism, and the Marxist basis of their thinking grew fainter. Remembering Jaspers's faith in

the great value of minds contending, even though no final
truth could ever be reached, it is revealing, and slightly
amusing, to read these words, written in 1944, by Adorno,
the subtlest of the members of the Frankfurt School and
Jaspers's former ideological opponent:

Nothing is more unfitting than for an intellectual to wish, in
discussion, to be right. The very wish to be right is an expression
of that spirit of self-preservation which philosophy is precisely
concerned to break down ... When philosophers, who are well
known to have difficulty in keeping silent, engage in conversation,
they should try always to lose the argument, but in such a way as
to convict their opponent of untruth. The point should not be to
have absolutely correct, irrefutable, watertight convictions – for
they inevitably boil down to tautologies – but insights which cause
the question of their justness to judge itself.

This came very close, in substance if not in style, to Hannah's
later position, as does this praise by Adorno, written at the
same time, of the intellectual's freedom from academic or
journalistic conformity: 'A gaze averted from the beaten
track, a hatred of brutality, a search for fresh concepts not
yet encompassed by the general pattern, is the last hope for
thought. In an intellectual hierarchy which constantly makes
everyone answerable, unanswerability alone can call the
hierarchy directly by its name.' This independence, this
unanswerability, was something Hannah was to maintain
all her life.

Yet at this moment she was particularly hostile to Adorno –
and for personal reasons, rather than because of the different
philosophical bases of their ideas. Günther Stern was invited
at Frankfurt to offer a thesis on the philosophy of music.

However, this was one of Adorno's special fields, and when Stern submitted a draft of his thesis, Adorno, who was one of the readers, rejected it.

Stern also had to face the fact that, even if he persevered with his *Habilitation*, the growing influence of the Nazis was making it more difficult all the time for a Jew to get a teaching post at a German university. In the event, he became a journalist, reporting on literary and cultural matters, with his first job in Berlin; and he went on writing journalism and fiction, under the name of Günther Anders, throughout a long life (he is still alive at the time of writing of this book, in 1985). But Hannah had no inclination to forgive Adorno for standing in the way of an academic career for her husband.

She herself had now got a small grant for research, and was beginning to study a new topic that interested her, the nineteenth-century German romantic poets and thinkers. She had also met again her grandfather's old friend, Kurt Blumenfeld, and under his guidance was beginning to take an interest in Zionism. The Nazis were forcing her at last to consider her own position as a Jewess in Germany. These new preoccupations were drawn closer together in her mind when she started to read the letters of a German Jewess who lived at the end of the eighteenth and the beginning of the nineteenth century, Rahel Varnhagen. And they led to the writing of her first book, apart from her doctoral thesis: a very curious biography called *Rahel Varnhagen: The Life of a Jewish Woman*.

Rahel was born, as Rahel Levin, in 1771, the daughter of a rich Jewish merchant in Berlin. In the liberal atmosphere of the time, she became a well-known Berlin figure, when as a young woman she held a salon in the attic of her parents' house, to which all the eminent Berlin intellectuals came. She had two intense but unhappy love-affairs, one with a very conventional German count, the other with a Spanish diplomat at the Legation. But the Napoleonic wars broke up her circle of friends, the German nobility grew more anti-Semitic, and Rahel began to feel more acutely the social disadvantage of being Jewish. She changed her name to Rahel Robert.

In 1814, when she was forty-three, she was baptized, and married August Varnhagen, a German who was fourteen years younger than she – an unsuccessful writer, a 'beggar by the wayside' as he called himself, who thought that with the inspiration of her brilliance and the help of her connections he could make a greater success of his life – as he did, eventually becoming a diplomat. Also, Rahel had written diaries and letters to her friends all her life, about her inner feelings and her friendships, and she allowed Varnhagen to publish parts of these, and win fame for himself through them. She never recovered her former position in German society, but before she died in 1833 she came to accept the Jewishness she had always tried to repudiate, especially after she had made friends with the young Jewish poet, Heinrich Heine, who wanted his voice, raised on behalf of the Jews, to 'ring resoundingly in the German beer-halls and palaces'. She declared her loyalty to her people, and identified herself with the cause of Jewish freedom and equality before the law. What had seemed to her the greatest shame and misery in her life, the fact of having been born a Jewess, appeared to her in the end as 'something she would on no account wish to have missed'.

Everyone who knew Hannah saw in this story a parable of her own life so far. She said the book was an attempt to tell Rahel's story as Rahel herself might have told it – but everywhere the words sound like Hannah's. Hannah does not try to create any background or atmosphere, or to bring to life any of the characters. All of these appear merely as part of Rahel's dense stream of thought, figures in her 'inner landscape' – except perhaps for Varnhagen himself, astounded by the world opened up to him by Rahel, hanging on to her doggedly, winning her by a mixture of slavish devotion and simple common sense.

Hannah Arendt first portrays Rahel as a girl entirely cut off from history: a young salon hostess in a world to which she in no way belonged, with only her empty, formal qualities – her intelligence and openness – to sustain her position outwardly; and only the whirl of her changing responses, and her endless, often desperate broodings on the nature of her rootless personality, to sustain her inwardly. This is certainly an exaggeration of Hannah's position in the German university milieu that she entered after she left home; but the account seems to tremble everywhere with feelings of intimate recognition on Hannah's part, as if she knew well enough from experience what she was writing about.

Rahel's first love-affair, with the count, means most to her as a chance to attach herself to some solid outer reality, to 'define herself from outside' and 'become a specific person'; her second love-affair, with the Spaniard, is on the contrary an attempt to submit herself completely to the magic of the man's beauty, and solve her problem that way. When she loses her lovers, the only positive thing left to her, with her lack of natural ties to the world, is her freedom. Did Hannah feel like this when she lost Heidegger? The passion with which she writes suggests that she did, however briefly.

But it is in the last part of the biography that we see most unmistakably an identity between Hannah and Rahel. Rahel does not love Varnhagen – but through marrying him she at last escapes the torment of having nothing in the world but that romantic possession, one's own personality. She acknowledges and welcomes the presence of brute reality in her life. And once she has been awoken in this way, she goes on to recognize how completely she had given herself up to all the insincerity and falsehood characteristic of the 'parvenu' in society – without ever having really succeeded in being part of it, merely accepted as an 'exception Jew' by the Germans. In the end she chooses the role of a 'conscious pariah', a woman who will not be an unquestioning member of educated society, nor completely outside it, but will hence-forth take an independent part, ambiguous in the most decent possible way: not repudiating society, but never forgetting or concealing her bond with those who are excluded from it. Here Rahel's position is described in terms that (as we have seen with 'parvenu' and 'pariah') Hannah Arendt made completely her own. And Rahel's resolutions, as an elderly lady, closely reflect a position which Hannah was now, in her mid-twenties, formulating for herself: to remain a part of German, and European, culture, but to be a 'conscious pariah' within it.

Hannah wrote *Rahel Varnhagen* in 1932 and 1933, except

for the last two chapters, which she finished in Paris in 1938 (the book was not actually published till 1958). No doubt when she wrote the end of the book her ideas had become clearer and firmer; but essentially they were the ones that were forming in her mind just before Hitler came to power.

The important fact was that in those years, in her own words, she 'opened her eyes' to the Jewish Question. 'From 1929 on,' Hans Jonas has said, 'it was quite clear that what one faced was the rise of Fascism. And my great surprise was when Hannah Arendt, my old friend, emerged as a figure in political science. That was essentially Hitler's deed. Up to then she had disdained the political sphere.'

Hannah did not join the German Zionist Organization, though Blumenfeld was its President. She sometimes feared a certain blinkered, sectarian emphasis in its activities, whereas she would have preferred it to act in awareness of the whole international political scene, where it was not only Jews who were in danger. She also had doubts about the 'Back to Palestine' policy, though that policy was not yet as important as it was to become later; certainly she herself had no desire to go and live in Palestine. But from this point on she 'accepted the Zionist critique of assimilation', as she put it – the view that assimilation meant the acceptance of anti-Semitism, whereas in fact the time had now come for Jews to stand up for the right of all Jews, no matter what their background, to live their lives as they chose under the guaranteed protection of the law. That, in some of her first journalism, and at public meetings, she began to express.

The other group in Germany who were most active in opposition to Hitler were the Marxists and Communists, who to begin with were in greater danger from the Nazis than the Jews were. Hannah knew many of them through Günther, whose friends in Berlin came mainly from these circles. But she was not drawn to their politics. The political stance she took up in this period was one that remained essentially the same for the rest of her life: she was always less concerned with material and social conditions than with political and legal rights. How her early political convictions of what was important to the Jews swelled into a majestic and far-ranging political philosophy, we shall eventually see.

1933, the year in which she was twenty-seven, was the turning-point in Hannah's life. Hitler's following had been growing steadily in Germany since the 1929 world slump and its consequent financial chaos; in the elections of March 1933, the National Socialists became the largest party in the German parliament, with 44 per cent of the votes. Hitler became the *Führer*, or Leader, of Germany. He had accused the Communists of plotting the fire in the Reichstag, or German parliament building, just before the elections, and he now began his reign of terror, in which Communists and supposed Communists were the first victims. Many were to be arrested, beaten and put into concentration camps. The boycott of Jewish businesses and the expulsion of Jews from official positions was also beginning.

Günther knew that his name was in an address book belonging to the left-wing poet and playwright, Bertolt Brecht, which was now in the hands of the Gestapo. He decided he must leave Germany. He and Hannah had grown steadily further apart in the previous two years, and his departure was the effective end of their marriage, though they later briefly shared a flat in Paris until their final separation.

Hannah turned her flat in Berlin into a refuge for fleeing Communists, masking their comings and goings with numerous visits from members of her family. She also started working for Blumenfeld and the German Zionists, compiling evidence of German anti-Semitism from the archives of the Prussian State Library. The fact that she was not a member of the Organization was an advantage here: if she were arrested, the Organization itself would not necessarily come under attack.

Before long, in fact, she was arrested, and held for questioning at police headquarters for eight days, in the spring of 1933. She managed to say nothing that would incriminate herself or the Organization, and even persuaded the policeman in charge of her to get cigarettes for her and improve the quality of the coffee. She was not frightened – but she knew it was time for her to go too.

She left Germany with her mother, illegally, across the Czech border, where there was a friendly house well known to the political Left, with its front door in Germany and its back door in Czechoslovakia. One idea was foremost in her thoughts. 'I wanted to do practical work,' she said in an interview after the war, 'exclusively and only Jewish work.' With that goal in mind, she made her way to Paris.

THREE

1933–41: Stateless in France

In her late twenties, Hannah still looked young, but her style was more severe now – her hair parted in the middle and brushed close to the sides of her long oval head, her clothes elegant but simple and strict in line. She looks at us steadily and calmly out of photographs of the time – but we know that, behind her clear brow, powerful new thoughts were already forming.

She and her mother went on from Czechoslovakia to Geneva, where Hannah got some temporary secretarial work at the League of Nations. But her mother, after the first alarms, had decided she wanted to return to her husband in Königsberg, which Hannah managed to arrange. Thus in the autumn of 1933 she arrived alone in Paris, and joined Günther Stern in his flat. She brought with her the manuscript of a novel – a satire on Fascism – that he had left behind in Berlin: it smelt richly of bacon, since it had been hidden in Berlin by being wrapped up in a cloth and hung among some smoked bacon in an attic. They went on living together, as friends, till Günther left for New York in 1936, after which they were formally divorced.

Hannah soon found another secretarial job when she got to Paris: this was at an organization called Agriculture et Artisanat, which trained young Jews in farming and the other skills they would need in order to emigrate to Palestine. But the overwhelming new fact in her life was her statelessness. In France, 'Europe's greatest immigration-reception area' as she called it, she was one of an enormous number of refugees and other aliens, all of them deeply confused about their rights and most of them fearful for their future. Hannah never wrote much in direct, personal terms about her own experiences of this kind; but the pages in *The Origins of Totalitarianism* about statelessness are among the most vivid and passionate in the book, and unmistakably convey to us some of her own strongest feelings. The discoveries she made at this time went on reverberating in her books to the end of her life.

She writes most keenly about the desperate feeling of the stateless person at having no rights at all, of being quite outside the pale of the law. With a kind of harsh wit, she describes how a stateless person may actually dream of committing a crime, just to 'improve his legal position ... Only as an offender against the law can he gain protection from it. The same man who was in gaol yesterday because of his mere presence in the world, who had no rights whatever and lived under threat of deportation, or who was dispatched without sentence and without trial to some kind of internment because he had tried to work and make a living, may become almost a full-fledged citizen because of a little theft. Even if he is penniless he can now get a lawyer, complain about his gaolers, and he will be listened to respectfully. He is no longer the scum of the earth but important enough to be informed of all the details of the law under which he will be tried. He has become a respectable person.'

In another part of the book, she speaks of the way in which 'professional idealists' with no political sense were liable to show their concern for the stateless: 'the groups they formed, the declarations they issued, showed an uncanny similarity in language and composition to that of societies for the prevention of cruelty to animals. No statesman, no political figure of any importance could possibly take them seriously; and none of the liberal or radical parties in Europe thought it necessary to incorporate into their programme a new declaration of human rights.' Hannah Arendt never had any time for sentimentalists.

All this led her to realize that the universal 'Rights of Man' that the eighteenth-century Enlightenment so proudly proclaimed had little meaning for a man unless he were an acknowledged member of a particular community; and that if he is that – even if he is a slave – he is still better off than a person who has 'lost a community willing and able to guarantee any rights whatsoever'. What all human beings need is a 'place in the world which makes opinions significant and actions effective'. It is only 'the loss of a polity itself that expels a man from humanity'.

The last bitter twist in these reflections on statelessness in her *Totalitarianism* book comes when she points out that to be stateless could – in spite of everything – sometimes be a person's goal. When the French premier, Pierre Laval, started expelling aliens from France in 1935, it was only people without a state to be deported to who were automatically exempt from the decree – and many people tried to establish for themselves the absence of status that was the only thing that would allow them to stay in France.

Hannah did not allow herself any self-pity when she was in Paris. At times she certainly knew despair; but she knew too that her lot was better than that of many of the refugees around her, and far better than that of many Germans, Jewish and Gentile alike, who were now in Hitler's concentration camps. What she did indefatigably was to learn from everything that happened to her and all that she saw. At least she had work that corresponded to her intentions when she left Germany – and in this respect she was even more fortunate when she went on to be given the post of *secrétaire-général* of the Paris office of a new organization, Youth Aliyah.

Youth Aliyah ('aliyah' means both 'ascending' and 'emigration (to Israel)') was an international body with similar aims to Agriculture et Artisanat. In Paris, it was mainly the children of new waves of refugees from Germany and Eastern Europe that came to the classes. But besides teaching them, Youth Aliyah also supervised the transport of its protégés to Palestine, where they were found homes in 'work villages'; and once, in 1935, Hannah was able to accompany a group by ship from Marseilles to Haifa, and to see Palestine for herself. She was very struck by the vigour and enthusiasm of the kibbutz workers – but just as interested in the relics of Greek and Roman civilization that she saw there. She could never envisage life in a Jewish state as the only proper destiny for Jews, and she was already afraid that a new Jewish nationalism might emerge there, with its own intolerance towards other races – the antithesis of everything that she herself thought was the proper destiny for Jews. But she also knew that henceforth she would feel a loyalty to this emerging Jewish state whose future citizens she was helping to prepare.

Meanwhile, in Paris, there was happiness to be found: no matter what her situation, some ebullient love of life was strong in her. Once, after the war, when William Phillips, an editor of *Partisan Review*, asked her why walking was so much easier in Paris than in New York, she replied with a laugh, 'The pavements are softer there.' If she was to be a refugee, at any rate Paris was the right place for it. In her essay on Walter Benjamin, included in the volume *Men in Dark Times*, she says: 'Paris had, with unparalleled naturalness, offered itself to all homeless people as a second home ever since the middle of the last century. Neither the pronounced xenophobia of its inhabitants nor the sophisticated harassment by the local police has ever been able to change this ... In Paris a stranger feels at home because he can inhabit the city the way he lives in his own four walls. And just as one inhabits an apartment by living in it instead of just using it for sleeping, eating and working, so one inhabits a city by strolling through it without aim or purpose, with one's stay secured by the countless cafés which line the streets and past which the life of the city, the flow of pedestrians, moves along ... What all other cities seem to permit only reluctantly to the dregs of society – strolling, idling, *flânerie* – Paris streets actually invite everyone to do. Thus, ever since the Second Empire the city has been the paradise of all those who need to chase after no livelihood, pursue no career, reach no goal – the paradise, then, of bohemians, and not only of artists and writers but all those who have gathered about them because they could not be integrated either politically – being homeless or stateless – or socially.'

Here – presented at its best – was the other side of the picture. There were many new friends to be made in Paris, particularly of the 'unintegrated' sort. Bertolt Brecht was now in Paris, and Hannah soon met him; she made the acquaintance of young French writers and thinkers like Jean-Paul Sartre and Raymond Aron. One of her oldest and closest friends from Königsberg, Anne Mendelssohn, was also there, married to a German, Eric Weil, who was a naturalized Frenchman (and who eventually fought for France). But it was Walter Benjamin himself whose friendship meant most to Hannah intellectually at this period, as the essay on him – one of the best things she ever wrote – reveals.

Benjamin was fourteen years older than Hannah, so he was in his forties when she knew him in Paris. He was another child of assimilated German Jews, trying like so many other such children to find a life with wider mental horizons than his parents', and a means of financing it. Hannah Arendt writes with intimate knowledge of this milieu when she describes the conflicts between these Jewish sons and their fathers: 'as a rule these conflicts were resolved by the sons' laying claim to being geniuses, or, in the case of the numerous Communists from well-to-do homes, to being devoted to the welfare of mankind – in any case, to aspiring to things higher than making money – and the fathers were more than willing to grant that this was a valid excuse for not making a living'. But in Benjamin's case, 'his father never recognized his claims, and their relations were extraordinarily bad'.

Arendt gives a very tender, gently humorous picture of the way this highly original, idiosyncratic literary critic was constantly thwarted in his attempts to make a regular living by 'the little hunchback' (*das bucklichte Männlein*) of the German children's rhyme, who is always knocking soup-pots or wine-jugs out of people's hands. When Benjamin tried to launch himself on a university career by writing a study of Goethe, he chose to attack a book by the very critic who could most have helped him; when he tried to improve his standing with the Frankfurt Institute of Social Research, where he had got a footing, by submitting an essay on Baudelaire for its magazine, he fell foul of Adorno, just as Günther Stern had done, for being insufficiently Marxist according to the Frankfurt School's own complex criteria. (However, Arendt conceded that Benjamin was probably 'the most peculiar Marxist' ever produced by the Frankfurt School – 'which God knows,' she adds tartly, 'has had its full share of oddities'.)

But she also draws out sympathetically the inner difficulties facing Benjamin. There was the classic German-Jewish dilemma of the time, so familiar to Hannah by now – whether to take part in German cultural life, and if so how, knowing what falsity a Jew might be drawn into by doing that. Arendt comments, 'For the Jews of that generation the available forms of rebellion were Zionism and Communism, and it is noteworthy that their fathers often condemned the Zionist rebellion more bitterly than the Communist.' But for Benjamin, like Hannah, neither way was really satisfactory: 'At the time when Benjamin tried, first, a half-hearted Zionism, and then a basically no less half-hearted Communism, the two ideologies faced each other with the greatest hostility:

the Communists were defaming Zionists as Jewish Fascists and the Zionists were calling the young Jewish Communists "red assimilationists".' What really attracted Benjamin to each of these movements was not so much its positive as its negative side, its 'criticism of existing conditions, a way out of bourgeois illusions and untruthfulness'. We hear, again, the unmistakable note of personal identification when Hannah adds that 'he was quite young when he adopted this radically critical attitude, probably without suspecting to what isolation and loneliness it would eventually lead him'.

What is most important in the end, though, is the recognition by Benjamin, as by Hannah Arendt, that with the rise of Hitler the 'dark times' were no longer just a problem for German Jews, but had engulfed all of Europe, and made a break with the whole Western political and moral tradition. (Indeed, she says unsparingly, Hitler put an end once and for all to the German-Jewish dilemmas.) She concludes the essay on Benjamin by describing his way, in his last writings, of coping with this desperate recognition; he became a kind of surrealist poet, making his work out of a montage of exquisite, unconnected quotations drilled up from the past, with no systematic vision to offer, but a capacity to startle and shock into new perceptions. This was certainly not to be Hannah Arendt's way, though she was as conscious by now of the 'break in tradition' as he was: yet she also went back, eventually, to ancient Greek ideas for a vision of politics against which present times could be measured, and from which they might draw fresh inspiration.

Benjamin was a significant figure for Hannah; but the most important person she met in Paris was not a renowned intellectual, nor a Jew. It was a man called Heinrich Blücher, a Communist refugee from Berlin, who was to become her second husband, and to whom she was to remain married for thirty years, until his death in New York in 1970.

She met him in the spring of 1936, when she was twenty-nine and he was thirty-seven. He was very unlike the solemn Heidegger, or the earnest Günther Stern. He was the son of a laundress from a Berlin suburb, and was amusing, impulsive, self-taught. He had fought with the Spartacists in Berlin in 1918 and 1919, and had been one of the first members of the German Communist Party, which had been formed during those battles; he had been a song-writer, a film critic, an amateur psychoanalyst. He had twice been married, and, though Hannah did not discover the fact for a while, was still married to his second wife at the time Hannah met him.

Above all, he was an impassioned and vivid talker. He and Hannah soon became lovers – Günther Stern had now left for New York – and slowly, responding both to his liveliness and his tact, she found herself being able to speak to him about feelings and fears she had never been able to acknowledge to Günther. She also found herself learning a great deal from him. He had a sense of history and politics that went far beyond the concerns of her Zionist friends. Later she was to acknowledge with unreserved gratitude the enormous influence on her own political thinking of this clever, un-tutored German who had learned his politics the hard way. And he told his friends that he had at last found the person he needed.

After this meeting, life in Paris took a new and better turn for Hannah. To the end of Heinrich's life she called him by the name 'Monsieur' – the way she had first heard him addressed by the concierge at his small Paris hotel.

But in the next two years, Jewish refugees in France had to contend with a growing mood of anti-Semitism. Their opposition to what was happening in Germany provoked particular hostility: they were accused of warmongering by those Frenchmen who hoped to avoid war by pacifying Hitler. Hannah's fighting spirit was only the more vigorously aroused: as in Germany at the beginning of the decade, she thought that the only policy possible for Jews was to speak up and protest, not to lie low in the hope that they would avoid persecution that way.

Her critical view of official Jewish organizations had already begun to form when she was still in Germany: now it became more pronounced. The Consistoire, the chief association of Paris Jews, was particularly anxious to keep Jews out of politics: Hannah saw it as a classic organization of those 'parvenus' whose attitude she had already so firmly rejected. (It was now that she wrote the last two chapters of *Rahel Varnhagen*.) After Hitler's annexation of Austria in March 1938, many more Jewish refugees arrived in France, and the French government began to take action against them, limiting the right of Jews to work, and trying to expel those without proper papers. This led to a fresh movement among many French and immigrant Jews to revert to the enclosed, community life of the ghetto. It was an impulse that Hannah considered completely ostrich-like, in the face of the steadily growing power and influence of Nazism in Europe.

In November 1938 came the grim night that was to be

remembered as the Kristallnacht, when the windows of Jews were smashed all over Germany, their homes looted, synagogues burned down and many Jews arrested. Hannah's mother decided to join her in Paris. Martin Beerwald, Hannah's stepfather, did not want to leave Königsberg; but Martha felt the need to be with her daughter. Of the stepsisters, Clara was dead – she had always had schizophrenic tendencies and had committed suicide in 1932; Eva had already gone to England, where she eventually found work as a technician in the manufacturing of dental material.

Martha left Königsberg in April 1939, and came to live with Hannah and Heinrich in a new flat they had taken. She did not like Blücher as much as she had liked Stern; but she urged them to get married, for practical reasons – if they were going to try to get a visa for the United States, it would be easier for them to stay together if they were a legally married couple. After the outbreak of war in September, Blücher was interned by the French authorities as a male German, but friends managed to get him released after a couple of months. He and Hannah both had their divorces by now, and they were married in Paris in January 1940. They were not to be together for long: in May, all refugees from Germany except old people and children were directed to labour or internment camps. The horrors of statelessness were growing plainer every day.

Hannah was taken to an internment camp at Gurs, on the Spanish border. She did not know where Heinrich had been sent. She got hold of some papers of release from the camp, in the chaos after the defeat of France in the following month,

and was taken in by some friends who had a house outside
Montauban. There was still no news of Heinrich. Then one
day, suddenly, she saw him in the main street of Montauban!
It was a joyful reunion. Heinrich had also got out of his camp
when France fell, and had come south with a great tide of
refugees. They found a small flat in Montauban; and that
summer, with their love of life still irrepressible, they bicycled
together all over the French countryside. Mary McCarthy
said to me, conveying the mood in which Hannah later
described those days: 'They had a ball!' Martha joined them
in the autumn. The South of France was now under the
French Vichy government,· which co-operated erratically
with the Germans; but, with a few narrow squeaks, all three
of them managed to accumulate the necessary visas to leave
France (Günther Stern helping from the American end), and
they crossed the Spanish frontier on a train bound for Lisbon
in January 1941.

Walter Benjamin was less lucky: the little hunchback
pursued him to the end. He had a Spanish transit visa, but
no French exit visa. There was a frontier post in the Pyrenees
where such refugees were allowed by the Spaniards to pass.
But on the day he tried, they had closed the frontier, and he
was ordered back into France. In despair, he killed himself.
Had he tried to cross the previous day, he would have got
through; had he left it till the next day, his group of refugees
would have known about the border closure, and all of them
would have waited for a better chance. As Hannah Arendt
wrote in her essay, 'only on that day was the catastrophe
possible'.

But Benjamin had given Hannah an important batch of

his manuscripts in the hope that she would get them through to his Frankfurt School friends in New York. She kept them as carefully as she had kept Stern's novel when she left Germany; and in due course, just as she had done with the novel, she delivered them safely to their destination.

FOUR

1941–51: A New Life in New York

Hannah and Heinrich arrived in New York by boat from Lisbon (Hannah always called it 'Lisboa') in May 1941. America was to be their home for the rest of their lives.

For a long time, life was very hard for them. They took two rooms on separate floors in a lodging-house in West 95th Street, one for themselves and one for Martha, who arrived from Portugal the following month. Here they lived for the next ten years, without even a kitchen of their own, only the communal house kitchen. But at the end of those ten years, the publication of Hannah Arendt's book *The Origins of Totalitarianism* was to make her famous.

Her book was maturing in many ways, simultaneously, throughout these years. The plight and the future of the Jews were still her chief preoccupation. As the war went on, the horrors of anti-Semitism in Germany were revealed more and more fully to the world, though many people – including the Blüchers themselves – could at first scarcely believe in them. Hannah's continuing historical study of anti-Semitism – and, now, of other forms of racism – seemed to take on a new and more dreadful significance with every revelation from the extermination camps. How had history come to this? And the future of the Jews after the war was a burning issue in America, with the dream of a Jewish state in Palestine gaining strength all the time. But what sort of state should it be, if its creation were possible? The war ended, and Stalin's totalitarianism, in turn, was exposed in all its cruelty. And in 1948 Israel was born, though not in the way that Hannah and her friends had hoped. The thought she gave to these and other events of the 1940s was to pour, in many guises, into the pages of *The Origins of Totalitarianism*.

At first, though, her task was to learn English and get a job. All the English she knew when she came to the States, she said, was 'two Shakespeare sonnets'; and Heinrich and Martha knew even less. A refugee organization arranged for her to spend two months with an American family in Massachusetts, where she had her first intimate glimpse of American life. The couple who took her in were very high-minded and puritanical; the wife allowed no smoking or drinking in the house, and they had a copy of Marie Stopes's *Ideal Love* on a shelf above their bed. In Hannah, though, they had taken in – in Mary McCarthy's words – 'a veritable hedgehog'; and she soon established her right to smoke in her bedroom, where the husband, hitherto banished to the garden for smoking, would come and join her in a cigarette. It was all very different from pre-war Paris or Berlin. Yet Hannah was impressed by the couple, especially their intense feeling for the democratic political rights and responsibilities of American citizens – both of these being demonstrated when Americans born in Japan were interned after the Japanese bombing of Pearl Harbor, and Hannah's hostess sat down immediately to write to her Congressman in protest. Hannah escaped before her two months' stay was up, however, by getting Heinrich to send her a telegram saying 'Mother extremely ill'.

For Heinrich and Martha, it was more difficult. Heinrich worked for a time shovelling chemicals in a factory; later he had a variety of jobs, researching into Nazi atrocities in order to publicize them in America, teaching German history to German prisoners-of-war, doing German-language broadcasting on NBC radio. But more and more he spent his time just reading and talking to Hannah, as they prepared the totalitarianism book. Martha, who was sixty-seven in 1941, cooked for them and managed to find some work making lace; but hers was the saddest and most isolated life, especially since the animosity continued between her and Heinrich, who thought that she was still trying – however ineffectually – to control Hannah's life.

Hannah had her first stroke of luck in the States in November 1941, when she got a job as a columnist on a German émigré newspaper, *Aufbau* ('Structure' or 'Construction'). It gave her a meagre living, and enabled her to start writing more than she had ever done before. The subject to which she first addressed herself in her articles was the formation of a Jewish army to fight alongside the Allies. For her, the Jews were above all a European people – more than that, indeed, they were 'good Europeans', who could see beyond purely national and class interests. She wanted them to assert themselves as a political body, and as upholders of a European tradition of freedom and justice. More practically, she was sure that if they joined in the fight against Hitler with an army of their own, it would help immeasurably in establishing their claim after the war to be recognized and consulted as a people – and their claim to their own homeland. On these topics she was soon writing with vigour and fire.

Nevertheless, her views began to diverge from the majority Jewish thinking in America – and even more from that of many Jews in Palestine. She condemned the Palestine terrorists, and their ambition to extend future Jewish territory east of the River Jordan. It was the same kind of Jewish nationalism, with the same disregard for Arab rights, that she had dissociated herself from in Germany in the 1930s – and she did not hesitate to call the terrorists and those who supported them 'Jewish Fascists'. Again, while American Zionists, inspired by David Ben-Gurion, were calling for the British to hand Palestine completely over to the Jews, she was developing the argument that Palestine should be a nation in which Jews and Arabs were equal citizens, and should become a member of the kind of British Commonwealth which seemed to her likely to develop after the war, with India a similar kind of 'dominion' member.

Thinking about these views, I am reminded of a description of Hannah Arendt by William Phillips, the *Partisan Review* editor, who met her soon after this time: he was impressed 'by the unusual combination of gentleness and force which, perhaps, was her most distinguishing trait to the end of her life. It was a very strange and seductive combination: firmness of tone and strength of conviction with a soft, almost caressing manner. Even at her most insistent, when she was rejecting an idea or a person and talking louder and more impatiently, her eyes always seemed to be smiling benignly.' One might say that her views on the formation of a Jewish army and on the future of Palestine reflect exactly that combination: they are firm in their assertion of Jewish rights, gentle in their notion of how Jews should behave towards others. But the combination was more seductive personally than politically. As history turned out, it was Hannah Arendt's opponents who were to prevail on both counts: British policy was against the idea of a Jewish army, so the American Zionist organizations soft-pedalled the proposal, for fear of annoying the American government by opposing an ally; whereas it was the nationalists, and even in some measure the terrorists, who determined the future shape of the state of Israel.

Hannah turned her efforts to supporting the Jewish cause in other ways. In 1944 she became the research director of a body called the Commission on European Jewish Cultural Reconstruction, whose purpose was to draw up a record of Jewish cultural treasures in the countries under Nazi rule, so that after the German defeat these monuments of the Jewish past could be recovered. In 1946 she began working as an editor in a New York publishing house, Schocken Books, founded by a friend of Blumenfeld's called Salman Schocken. Her main achievement here was to bring out a beautifully edited German edition of Kafka's diaries, from a manuscript prepared by Kafka's friend Max Brod which needed innumerable corrections because of Brod's carelessness. In 1948 she became the executive director of Jewish Cultural Reconstruction; and she went to Europe the following year in order to supervise the recovery of vast numbers of Jewish books, ceremonial artefacts and law scrolls, and to find suitable homes for them in Israel, and in Europe and America.

But as the war approached its end, the most pressing question for her was whether she could begin to write in English. Little by little she had begun to meet American writers – especially the group connected with *Partisan Review*, which had been started in the 1930s as a pro-Communist journal; the review's editors, William Phillips and Philip Rahv, reacted sharply, however, against Stalin's Communism and had by this time turned it into the leading liberal intellectual journal in the USA. Phillips and Rahv were constantly at loggerheads with each other – Rahv was notorious for his acid criticisms of all his closest friends, which he once justified as 'analytic exuberance' – but between them they had mustered many of the best new American writers as regular contributors – poets like Randall Jarrell and Robert Lowell, novelists like Mary McCarthy – and they also brought in many European writers, like George Orwell during the war and Sartre and Camus soon after it ended.

Here was a milieu in which Hannah could feel at home, though she was instinctively careful to guard her independence among them. One of the *Partisan* staff of the time, William Barrett, has described how they, too, welcomed the acquaintance with Hannah. They were, he says, a 'little band of intellectuals waiting for the cultural news from Europe', and Hannah Arendt would become their interpreter of it: 'she was always conscious of coming from elsewhere – of speaking for something older and deeper that she understood as European culture, something that she guarded at her centre. So that for us she became a kind of incarnation of the European presence that began to be felt more and more in New York in the 1940s.' Another new friend of that time, the critic Alfred Kazin, has expressed a similar feeling very vividly:

'I met Hannah Arendt in 1946, at a dinner party ... She was a handsome, vivacious forty-year-old woman who was to charm me and others, by no means unerotically, because her interest in her new country, and for literature in English, became as much a part of her as her accent and her passion for discussing Plato, Kant, Nietzsche, Kafka, even Duns Scotus, as if they all lived with her and her strenuous husband Heinrich Blücher in the shabby rooming house on West 95th Street.'

Helen Wolff, another publisher, who got to know her when they met to discuss business at Schocken Books, gives a more intimate picture:

'She was always direct, played no games, was above manipulation. She had a disarming way of saying "Okay, okay" when she gave in to an argument, used Berlin jargon, called grown men *"Kindchen"* and generally seemed at ease with the world.'

But the most important new friendship that Hannah made now, one which was to last until Hannah's death, was with Mary McCarthy. They did not become friends immediately, as often happens with such strong personalities. They were first introduced to each other in a New York hotel bar by the art critic, Clement Greenberg – another *Partisan* figure – in 1943. They met again at one of Philip Rahv's Friday-night parties the following year, when the French were rising up in arms against the retreating Germans. As Mary McCarthy arrived, she said ironically but provocatively, 'I feel sorry for Hitler.' Hannah turned to her husband and asked him to take her home immediately, observing: 'How can she say that to someone who has been in a concentration camp?'

However, they went on seeing each other as members of the editorial board of another magazine, *politics*, edited by the ebullient Dwight Macdonald. Hannah would still not speak directly to Mary McCarthy; but they repeatedly found them- selves expressing similar views on questions that came up. One day, two years after the incident at Rahv's, they walked back together down to the subway station, where Hannah suddenly said: 'Let's stop this, shall we? We always agree, and we always agree against everyone else. Also – I have a confession to make. I was never in a concentration camp.' She had of course been in an internment camp, and she had felt, at that moment, that she could make the claim she did in order to speak on behalf of all Jews. With this avowal, the long-lasting and close friendship between the two women began.

Hannah Arendt's first article in *Partisan Review* was a 're-evaluation' of Kafka, published in the autumn of 1944. Soon she started contributing articles on political history and thought that were to become sections of *The Origins of Totalitarianism*. She wrote in English, and William Phillips helped her to make corrections and polish the language – not cramping, but bringing out, her forceful, often epigrammatic style. By 1946, she was contributing to other American journals, including the *Sewanee Review*, the *Nation* and *Commentary*: many of these pieces also contained material that was to appear in her book. A young woman called Rose Feitelson, who liked the company of New York writers and intellectuals and gave parties for them in Greenwich Village, became Hannah's regular 'Englisher'. Hannah was also lecturing, both at Brooklyn College and at an institution set up by German émigrés, the New School for Social Research.

But the book was her main concern now. Something of the passion behind it appears in a short article which she wrote for a German-language magazine, *Die Wandlung* ('Change'), as early as 1944, and which appeared in translation in *Jewish Frontier* the following year: 'Organized Guilt and Universal Responsibility'. Her life in New York was becoming more settled, and there was a little more money to spend, at last, on making their conditions easier; but she was not giving up the voice of the 'pariah'. Here she lashed out at those 'good family men' and 'job-holders' who had acquiesced in the Nazi horrors under the pressure of the regime. The family man, she said, was 'the greatest criminal of the century'. The 'caring father, concerned above all for security' had been transformed into 'an adventurer who with all his anxiety could never be sure of the next day . . .' And it had turned out that such men were 'willing to sacrifice conscience, honour and human dignity for the sake of pension, life-insurance, the secure existence of wife and children'. This article did not form a part of the book, but one of its key themes is boldly and harshly announced in it.

Later, in a way that may perhaps be seen as a comment on the savage tone of this article, Hannah wrote that the years 1945 to 1949, 'the years I spent writing *The Origins of Totalitarianism*, seem in retrospect like the first period of relative calm after decades of turmoil, confusion and plain horror'. It began to be possible in those years to look on contemporary events 'still in grief and sorrow and, hence, with a tendency to lament, but no longer in speechless outrage and impotent horror'. The book was published – a book of a quarter of a million words – in the United States early in 1951; in Great Britain it came out later in the year, under the title *The Burden of Our Time*. What had Hannah Arendt tried to do in this sorrowing distillation of so much of her thought and experience in her life so far?

The starting point in the conception – and the finishing point in the narrative – of *The Origins of Totalitarianism* is the Nazi extermination camps. Hannah Arendt portrays the terror and the genocide for which those camps were created as the necessary goal of the whole whirling, on-driving movement of Nazi totalitarianism. And she wants to ask: how did these unforseeable and previously unimaginable horrors appear in man's history? Can we begin to understand this unspeakable outrage to all our once-cherished conceptions of man's dignity – or at least of man's elementary rationality and common sense?

Hannah Arendt did not believe that any simple causal explanations of history were possible. No human action, she thought, is wholly explicable in the light of what has gone before, even with hindsight. Yet events could create at least a predisposition in people to behave in certain ways, or make it easier for them to do so. In the first two sections of her book, Arendt ranges far and wide through the history of the last 200 to 300 years, identifying events that might be thought to have played that kind of part in the eventual emergence of totalitarianism. The book at one time had the provisional title *Three Pillars of Hell*: the first two 'pillars', which are the respective subjects of these two sections, are 'Anti-Semitism' and 'Imperialism' (the third pillar was to have been 'Racism', but it becomes incorporated into the 'Imperialism' section). These investigations are wonderfully rich in fact and in speculation. Both author and reader are sometimes swept away by the sheer fascination of the subject; but the goal is never lost sight of.

Hannah Arendt sets the scene with the nation-states of Europe as they developed at the end of the feudal era. Here was a world of legitimate and limited conflicts: within each nation, conflicts between class and class and between party and party; in Europe as a whole, conflicts between one nation and another, without the wish on the part of any of them to destroy the 'comity of nations'.

Arendt's opening question is : how, in this Europe, did anti-Semitism first take hold? Arendt does not blame the Jews for the hostility shown to them at different times and places; but she insists, calmly and dispassionately, that it was often intelligible. She will not accept the view that Jews became wholly arbitrary scapegoats for angry passions that had nothing at all to do with them; nor will she accept that modern anti-Semitism is simply the continuation of an ancient conflict between Jew and non-Jew, without any special precipitating circumstances. Either view she regards as, in fact, diminishing to Jews, taking away from them their responsibility for their place in the world.

Jews came to the fore in much of Europe as bankers to the royal courts and the aristocracy. Some of them achieved high social positions. But in the nineteenth century, as she sees the story, monarchs and governments began to turn more

and more to the new capitalist bourgeoisie for their financial
needs, while the bourgeoisie in turn began to play a greater
part in government; and wealthy Jews lost their special
function. But now they stood out even more conspicuously
in society, having money but no obvious power or usefulness;
and this provoked resentment from all classes. 'Such conditions', she says, 'cut all the threads which bind men together. Wealth which does not exploit lacks even the
relationship which exists between exploiter and exploited;
aloofness without policy does not imply even the minimum
concern of the oppressor for the oppressed.'

These anti-Jewish feelings were not precisely the same as
those that Hitler later expressed, and inflamed in the German
people; but they developed into a European legacy of hostility
that helped to prepare the way for him. And the Jews did not
protect themselves as a body against such hostility, divided
as they were between those successful Jews who still wanted
a role in the upper reaches of society (many of them in fact
becoming admirable artists and thinkers) and the majority
who withdrew into their traditions and took no part in the
political or social life of the country they lived in. (It is
here that Arendt draws her important distinction between
'parvenus' and 'pariahs'; we have also seen how the lack of
a political sense was something she was still reproaching the
Jews with during the 1939–45 war.)

Into this argument she inserts vivid accounts of particular
episodes that illustrate it in oblique ways: the rise to power
in Great Britain of Benjamin Disraeli, who made the most of
the idea that the Jews were a people apart, turning it to his
advantage as a source of glamour and mystery for himself

among non-Jews, however little that helped his own people; and the Dreyfus case in France at the end of the nineteenth century, which brought out against the supposedly unpatriotic Jews the 'mob', the flotsam of rootless and violent inhabitants of the cities, in a way that much more closely anticipated what was to happen at first in Nazi Germany – though the episode ended swiftly and farcically when the French nation turned its attention to making a success of the 1900 Paris Exhibition. (In fact, for the Jews, the most lasting effect of the case was that it gave birth to the Zionist movement.)

After this provocative and ironical excursion into the history of anti-Semitism, Hannah Arendt turns her attention to the second – and perhaps rather more unexpected – pillar of the hell which Europe was to enter in the 1930s: 'Imperialism'. Here she discovers a far more pervasive effect on the world atmosphere in which the totalitarian regimes were to find their chance. She shows how European imperial expansion left behind it a more flagrant breach with established traditions of justice, and a more devastating assault on the rights of man, than the European peoples had yet been guilty of. But, she argues, Europe itself was to be, in the end, the victim of this disregard for its own political ideals.

As with the rise of modern anti-Semitism, we go back, to begin with, to an economic change: the fact that in late nineteenth-century Europe, with the rapid growth of the continent's industrial production, there was suddenly a superabundance of capital. Britain, France, Germany and Belgium looked overseas to use that capital, taking over vast new territories in order to do so: the years 1884 to 1914, the years of imperialism, were 'a period of stagnant quiet in Europe and breathtaking developments in Asia and Africa'. Cecil Rhodes expressed the moving principle of the new era when he said 'Expansion is everything', then 'fell into despair every night he saw overhead "these stars . . . these vast worlds which we can never reach. I would annex the planets if I could."'

Arendt portrays the whole history of imperialism as one of 'inherent insanity and contradiction to the human condition'. As Rhodes had willingly shown, there was no intelligible goal, no point at which a rational purpose would have been achieved: merely expansion because there was, now, the possibility of expansion. Here was a clear anticipation of the totalitarian state of mind.

In the way the great new colonies were governed, other precedents were set. The new imperial rule consisted neither of limited, *ad hoc* conquest and exploitation, of which men had always been guilty; nor of the incorporation of the colonies into the polity of the ruling nation (except in the case of France, where, Arendt says, the only effective outcome was the death of innumerable black troops in French armies). Enormous lands now came under complete rule not by law but by decree: their natives were classified as inferior citizens on the mere basis of their race or colour. Of course, there was opposition to these policies in Europe, with unhappy politicians ranged against enthusiastic businessmen; but, in Arendt's fine, Roman-sounding phrase, 'the only grandeur of imperialism lies in the nation's losing battle against it'. She acknowledges that many colonial administrators, especially British ones, worked hard for the welfare of the native people, often feeling themselves to be better examples of their own national decency – 'heroic servants of the nation' – than 'the people back home'. But this was still the rule of inferior by superior and actually exacerbated the sense of racial difference on both sides.

Arendt gives some brilliant sketches of types who went out to the colonies in these years: the dispossessed aristocrats and the rootless men of the 'mob', allied now on the only social footing they had, that of being members of the white race; the noble but absurd adventurers like Lawrence of Arabia, who could only find a meaning for his life in the Great Game of world politics, which overrode all normal human considerations; the British administrator, 'who no longer believed in the universal validity of law, but was convinced of his own innate capacity to rule and dominate'. With these, she says, 'the stage seemed to be set for all possible horrors. Lying under anybody's nose were many of the elements which gathered together could create a totalitarian government on the basis of racism.'

Back in Europe, imperialism was having yet further effects, bringing the continent itself closer to Nazism and Bolshevism. The Pan-German and Pan-Slav movements were growing in the nations of Central and Eastern Europe, especially Austria and Russia. They had received a great impetus from the 'triumphant imperialist expansion of the Western nations in the 1880s' : the feeling was increasing that these nations 'had the same right to expand as other great peoples, and if they were not granted this possibility overseas they would be forced to do it in Europe'. The real opportunity for expansion was of course negligible; but such ideas appealed especially to the rootless, mob element in Europe, and it was not long before this new 'tribal nationalism' started looking for enemies and finding them in the Jews. Here lay the beginnings of late nineteenth- and twentieth-century anti-Semitism – reviving latent feelings inherited from history, no doubt, but taking a new and more virulent form, racist in a blind and undiscriminating way. The Jews could be seen as a tribe without boundaries, just like the Slavs and the Germans – but an enemy one. This kind of nationalism was hostile to parties and party governments, preferring authoritative leaders and rule by decree.

The First World War provides the finishing touches to Hannah Arendt's picture of the 'origins of totalitarianism'. In its wake came inflation, bankruptcy and unemployment, and another great swelling of the ranks of the displaced and hopeless, ready to snatch at any satisfaction. The creation of the new, smaller nations of Europe produced everywhere discontented minorities who looked for support not to their own government but to members of their race beyond the frontier. Innumerable people moved in fear – or were moved by force – into countries of exile where they remained stateless (Arendt's haunting description of statelessness, quoted earlier, comes at this point); and Europe grew used to the idea that there were people without rights, whom governments could freely harass or expel. Governments themselves became – as we have seen happening in Weimar Germany – objects of contempt, in this chaotic situation that they could not control.

So we come to the third section of the book, 'Totalitarianism'. Here, Hannah Arendt does not attempt to give a stage-by-stage history of Hitler's or Stalin's rise to supreme power; rather, she shows in a more abstract way how in their systems the essential elements of totalitarianism came together or 'crystallized'.

For her, the fundamental precondition for the success of Nazism is the appearance in Europe of the 'mass man'. Beyond the comparatively small 'mob' of the wholly uprooted were, as Arendt describes them, the masses: great numbers of atomized, isolated individuals, without any distinct feeling of belonging to a group or class, longing to escape from the arbitrary, unintelligible course of their daily life into 'the fictitious consistency of an ideology'. Totalitarianism lures these unattached masses into loyalty by its megalomaniac propaganda, offering world domination as a goal to them, and providing enemies to fear and hate on all sides; simultaneously, it terrorizes them into loyalty by the use of ruthless and arbitrary murder.

It claims to represent no specific group, or in the early stages to represent all groups: the name of the Nazis, the Nationalist Socialist German Workers' Party, 'offered a synthesis supposed to lead to national unity, a semantic solution whose double trademark of "German" and "Worker" connected the nationalism of the Right with the internationalism of the Left'. Hitler found Germany already well on the road to an 'atomized' condition; Stalin had to destroy classes and parties – and finally the only group left, his own bureaucracy – by purges and slaughter; in the end, both had what they wanted, a malleable mass without any impulse to turn anywhere other than to their Leader.

Equally, totalitarianism offers no clear or specific programme – because that might lead to a goal achieved, a halt, a relaxation. As with late nineteenth-century imperialism, movement and expansion is its endless purpose. Its one ultimate ambition is the total domination of man, which entails the destruction of any moral sense both in its followers and its victims, and the perpetual murder of men in order to re-establish continually that domination and to preserve the ongoing force of the movement. The Jews could instantly be chosen as the first enemies to overcome: they could be portrayed as engaged in a worldwide conspiracy against the German people. Once that had been established, their elimination gave a momentum to Nazism that could go on and on as long as a single Jew remained alive. In Arendt's view, Hitler welcomed the Second World War less for the opportunity it gave for the extension of German territory, than for the renewed fanaticism it would inspire in the matter of Jew-killing and the new energy which that would create in the Nazi ranks. In one of her most graphic phrases, Arendt describes totalitarianism as a movement of 'superfluous men attempting to make men superfluous'.

The ultimate motivating force behind the whole hideous phenomenon of totalitarianism is seen by Arendt as an impulse in its leaders that she can only describe as 'radical evil'. It was a desire to convert the whole universe into the material of their private fantasy, rejoicing in the abandonment of any restraint that might limit that fantasy, actually revelling in the killing of a race or other enormous group that they had conjured up as their enemies, proving to their satisfaction that any deed, no matter how unimaginably horrific hitherto, was possible to them.

The Origins of Totalitarianism offers no tightly knit story of historical cause and effect to explain the rise of Nazism and Stalinism; nor does it have anything to say about the final, precipitating force in the psychology of men like Hitler and Stalin other than to evoke that radical evil in them. Yet as we read the book, the whole nightmare is re-enacted for us before our eyes, in a way that makes it seem correct to say that we have begun to understand it.

The book made a great impact in America. More than any other work of political science or journalistic report, more than any personal memoirs, it seemed to bring the events of the previous twenty years in Europe into focus. But it was also much criticized. Orthodox historians and political scientists, valuing thorough documentation and a careful, empirical treatment of fact, thought that its sweeping, often very abstract approach to such difficult matters was unrewarding and misleading. This was particularly the case with the sections on Stalinism – which Hannah admitted were based on a less familiar acquaintance with the subject than her much more substantial treatment of Nazism. Isaiah Berlin, a lifelong critic of Hannah Arendt, approaching political history as he does in that English and American empirical tradition, said to me, no doubt with a touch of conscious mischief, 'She doesn't get a single fact about Russia right.'

The sections on Stalinism also provoked criticism from a very different quarter. In drawing the comparisons she does between Hitler and Stalin, Arendt was accused by many left-wing and even liberal writers of vilifying the aims of Communism and inflaming the Cold War, at a moment when a more sympathetic understanding of Russia was particularly needed. There was Jewish criticism of the book, too; although it had been inspired by the fate of the Jews in Germany, it did not portray them in a particularly warm or heroic light.

Nevertheless, to read it today is still to undergo a profound experience. It is a harrowing book, and a grim warning that seems as relevant as ever about the human tendency to fall into belief in cruel and self-serving myths – with the constant danger of cruel and insane myths swallowing up even those. Alfred Kazin has said that the account of totalitarianism itself in the final section has the force of 'a stupendous literary idea, like the structure of Dante's Hell'. That remark can stand, and does not diminish the book: whatever its factual inaccuracies, it has the truth to human experience that we find in literature. Also, the glimmers and flickers of normal human life that occasionally appear in the darkness have a poignancy that is strangely inspiring. The conflicts of men going about their normal, intelligible business become acceptable, even an object of nostalgia, set against the totalitarian universe of endless, meaningless violence. A passing remark Arendt makes about Lawrence of Arabia – he lacked 'the calm good conscience of some limited achievement' – hurls one back into the life Hannah herself had succeeded in maintaining throughout these years. And in her conclusion – a chapter she added in 1953, two years after the book's first publication – she turned the totalitarian dream on its head. If 'everything was possible' to man, as the Nazis had tried to show by taking evil to its last extremes, then something else was possible, too – a new beginning:

HANNAH ARENDT

'Beginning is the supreme capacity of man; politically, it is identical
with man's freedom. *Initium ut esset homo creatus est* —
"that a beginning be made man was created," said Augustine.
This beginning is guaranteed by each new birth; it is indeed every
man.'

FIVE

1951–58: The Human Condition

In 1951, the year of *The Origins of Totalitarianism*, Hannah finally received American citizenship. Heinrich's citizenship followed in 1952. Both of them were profoundly grateful for it. Hannah would often criticize America in later years – but she would also discover, in its Founding Fathers, an embodiment of the ideal of political freedom that was to be the subject of her next book, *The Human Condition*. She treasured in the United States the opportunity that Jews and other naturalized immigrants had to exercise full political rights, without having to pretend that they were other people than they really were. Here it was not necessary for a Jew to choose between being a parvenu or a pariah: one could be both an American citizen, and loyal to one's origins, without any conflict.

Martha's second husband, Martin Beerwald, had died of a stroke in 1942. His death had come in an old people's home in a part of Königsberg to which Jews had been restricted; but he had not suffered at Nazi hands. Martha herself had died in 1948, in sad circumstances. She had decided to go to London to live with her stepdaughter, Eva. She sailed for

England on the *Queen Mary*; but she died on board ship.

Hannah grieved; but Heinrich could not help showing his relief that he and Hannah would now be alone together. In a letter he wrote to her at this time, he judged Martha harshly for what he thought she had done to Hannah: 'It made me furious, her constant blood-sucking of you and her total lack of respect for your unbelievable work ... Nonetheless, you are surely correct: there was once in her a true, great and clear feeling, which was finally dissolved into a mass of muddy sentimentalities.' However it was he, more than Hannah, who felt liberated by her death; Hannah had been quite strong enough to create the freedom she wanted for herself. Blücher began reading and thinking again with almost manic vigour, and soon got a chance to start lecturing about his newly developed ideas on art and history at the Eighth Street Club, an artists' club in Greenwich Village. That led in due course to paid teaching jobs at the New School and at Bard College.

Soon after Martha's death, Heinrich also began a love-affair with a younger woman who was a friend of both his and Hannah's. It was something that Hannah found hard to accept; but the marriage was more important to her. She and Heinrich went on living together with a new degree of independence, and a pledge that there would be no secrets between them. One of their new American friends, the poet Randall Jarrell, later drew a portrait of the Blüchers in his novel, *Pictures from an Institution*, where he called them the Rosenbaums. He described their marriage as a 'Dual Monarchy': a wholly equal but deeply united couple, standing up passionately to each other for their ideas and concealing none of them, but always attentive about providing little pleasures and signs of love.

Hannah herself had gone on a romantic pilgrimage in 1949, when she visited Europe for Jewish Cultural Reconstruction. She stayed with Karl Jaspers and his wife Gertrud in Basle – and then she went on in January 1950 to see Martin Heidegger in Freiburg.

Jaspers, married to a Jewess, and refusing to co-operate in any way with the Nazis, had been banned from all academic work or publishing after 1938; the American army arrived in Heidelberg in 1945 just in time to save him and his wife from what the Nazis called 'deportation'. He had held steadfast to his convictions throughout these years, and had become a new inspiration to those Germans who wanted to rebuild Germany as a democratic nation. For Hannah, hearing from him in 1945 had helped to restore the continuity between the lost past and a future she might believe in; when she met him in his new house in Basle in December 1949 she at once felt herself at home, both personally and philosophically. When he received the German Peace Prize in 1958, she was asked to give the address in his honour at the award ceremony in Frankfurt, and she said:

'It was self-evident that he would remain firm in the midst of catastrophe. But that the whole thing could never become even a temptation for him – this, which is less self-evident, was his inviolability, and to those who knew of him it meant far more than resistance and heroism. It meant a confidence that needed no confirmation, an assurance that in times in which everything could happen one thing could not happen. What Jaspers represented then, when he was entirely alone, was not Germany but what was left of *humanitas* in Germany. It was as if he alone in his inviolability could illuminate that space which reason creates and preserves between men, and as if the light and breadth of this space would survive even if only one man were to remain in it ...'

The meeting with Heidegger had been very different. Heidegger had believed, at least for a time, that Nazism offered some prospect of a return in Germany to that deep 'responsiveness to Being' that he sought; he had joined the Nazi Party, and was appointed Rector of Freiburg University by them in 1933. He spoke publicly of 'the nobility of this public awakening', and he forbade his own former professor, Husserl, to enter the university because he was a Jew. He never subsequently retracted these opinions, simply fell silent about them; from 1945 to 1951 he was forbidden to teach by the Allied authorities in Germany, though he offered to put himself at their disposal for the 're-education' of the German people. Hannah, in her article on *Existenz* philosophy in *Partisan Review* in 1946, had made a caustic comment about the 'real comedy' of this offer of Heidegger's. But she had added, unable to suppress the tenderness and urge to forgive that she still felt for him: 'Heidegger is, in fact, the last (we hope) romantic', whose 'complete irresponsibility' could be attributed 'partly to the delusion of genius, partly to desperation'.

Heidegger still called out to the sense of romance and drama in Hannah. When she got to Freiburg, she sent him an unsigned message from her hotel, simply saying 'I am here'. And as she must have hoped, he not only knew who it was but came to her immediately. For him, it turned out, she was exactly what she had been twenty-five years before – he hardly seemed aware of anything that had happened in those years that might have come between them. Hannah knew that there could be no future in the relationship; but she decided after this meeting that she was right never to have forgotten, and she always kept a photograph of him on her desk afterwards in New York.

Now, though, in 1951, with her first book successfully behind her, a new phase of life was beginning for her and Heinrich. They finally gave up their rooms on West 95th Street, and took an apartment in Morningside Drive, where they would each have a room of their own to work in. Slowly it filled up with the heavy, Biedermeier-style furniture that had surrounded them both in their youth. Hannah had a Guggenheim Fund grant to help her get on with her new book, and she also began to receive invitations to lecture at American universities. In 1953 she gave a set of lectures on 'Marx and the Great Tradition' for the Christian Gauss Seminars in Criticism that took place at Princeton; in 1955 she gave a series of lectures on political history at Berkeley.

She had defended the sections about Russian totalitarianism in her book partly on the grounds that totalitarianism was a distinct phenomenon that might recur, in twentieth-century world conditions, in different countries: if that were so, as she feared, it was more important to be alert to the essential similarities between manifestations of totalitarianism than to dwell on their less significant differences. In the 1950s, she was particularly concerned with the indications that totalitarianism could declare itself in the United States.

The Origins of Totalitarianism had, as we have seen, been regarded by some political writers – on both sides – as a contribution to the Cold War. Hannah Arendt herself continued to regard Stalin, in his last years, as a totalitarian ruler – the more so, when anti-Semitism began to play a growing part in Stalinist policy. 'The open and unashamed adoption of the most prominent sign of Nazism was', she subsequently observed, 'the last compliment Stalin paid to Hitler, his late colleague and rival in total domination.'

What, however, with perfect consistency, she feared in the United States in the early 1950s was the growing tendency on the Right to fight totalitarianism with totalitarian methods. In an article published in 1953, she said, 'If you try to "make America more American" or a model of democracy according to any preconceived idea, you can only destroy it.' The main villain was, of course, Senator Joe McCarthy, with his campaign against 'un-American activities'. But she was also anxious about the influence of the ex-Communist intellectuals – some of whom were friends and acquaintances – who were attacking what she considered basic civil liberties in magazines like *Commentary*. 'The limitations on dissent', she wrote, 'are the Constitution and the Bill of Rights and no one else.' She was already speaking as a confident and clear-eyed American citizen.

Her own thinking was taking a new course. It was as if, after years of unhappy preoccupation, both mental and practical, with twentieth-century attempts to destroy human freedom, she wanted to draw now a picture of perfect freedom as she would conceive it. *The Human Condition*, her next book, which was published in 1958, concludes with such a picture – though it is approached and defined through another study of its opposites.

Hannah had intended to write a book about Karl Marx – in particular, a study of the role played by Marxism in the development of Soviet totalitarianism. It was an area she felt she had not paid enough attention to in the *Totalitarianism* book; typically – and unlike her critics, such as Isaiah Berlin – she thought the weakness in the book was not its shortage of ordinary historical fact, but its inadequate attention to a particular set of ideas! These new Marx studies were the basis of her Princeton lectures in 1953 – but they led her away from her original plan, as she began to see aspects of Marxism that struck her with a new force.

Her main 'discovery' – for herself, at least – was the distinctive way in which Marx had challenged all previous political traditions in the West. This was not in fact a break on the lines of Hitler's or Stalin's evil intervention in history; it sprang, rather, from the supreme importance that Marx gave to labour and production in human life. Marx had indeed not so much broken with tradition as stood it on its head. He was not in the least a conscious forerunner of the totalitarian leaders; on the contrary, he held the traditional belief that freedom was one of the greatest human values. But whereas, in earlier Western thought, labour and production were seen as the realm in which man was most bowed and bent by necessity, and felt least free, Marx saw human labour as 'the expression of the very humanity of man'. He glorified human labour, which distinguished man from the animals and enabled him to create a world of abundance. Freedom for all men would come, as Marx saw it, when their labour was truly valued and they all received the full fruits of it. Man would be 'socialized'; society would be equitably administered; the state, even politics itself, would wither away, because man's freedom would have been achieved.

It was a vision of happiness – yet Hannah Arendt saw it as both a delusion and a nightmare. A delusion, because what in fact had happened with the supposed 'emancipation of labour', both in socialist and capitalist countries, was not 'an age of freedom for all', but the growing prospect of 'all mankind being forced for the first time under the yoke of necessity'. And a nightmare, because even if the utopia as Marx saw it could ever be achieved, it would leave men with nothing to do but consume. It would give them no scope for challenge, for brave, bold political action: their freedom, compared with what Hannah Arendt conceived of as freedom, would be a worthless one. 'What else is this ideal,' she wrote, 'but the age-old dream of the poor and destitute, which can have a charm of its own so long as it is a dream, but turns into a fool's paradise as soon as it is realized?'

This was the background to *The Human Condition*. But the book itself is based on an earlier story: the story of life, work and politics in the Ancient Greek city-states, as Hannah Arendt pieced it together imaginatively for herself from the works of the Greek poets, historians and philosophers. Mirrored in the first civilized world of which we have anything like a proper record, she saw the essential features of the 'condition' under which men, finding themselves in this world, always have to live.

When it was published, the poet W. H. Auden said: 'Every now and then, I come across a book which gives the impression of having been especially written for me ... It seems to answer precisely those questions which I have been putting to myself ... Miss Hannah Arendt's *The Human Condition* belongs to this small and select class.' Sheldon Wolin, the professor of politics at Princeton, looking back after Hannah's death to the time of the book's appearance, said that, before it, political theory was just 'a special branch of the history of ideas, neither political nor theoretical'; *The Human Condition* came 'as a deliverance in 1958 to those who were trying to restate a conception of political theory relevant to the contemporary world ... it brought something new into the world.' But this 'something new' was not all that easy to interpret: we shall try now to disentangle what the book's message was.

Her subject is not, she says, the whole of man's life: she is leaving out what was perhaps most important of all for the Greeks, the life of thought, the *vita contemplativa*. Her subject here is the life of activity, the *vita activa*. In the Greek city-state, she sees the three fundamental elements in all human activity most clearly articulated: they are, respectively, labour, work and action – the last two of these words having a special meaning, as we shall see in a moment.

As she reconstructs it, the ancient Greek world kept labour, or the production of necessities – and its counterpart, consumption – out of sight. These activities were all carried out in the home: slaves did the labour, the family consumed in private. This was men's sphere in so far as they were mere creatures of nature toiling for survival, the *animal laborans*.

There was a nobler form of production – work, or craftsmanship, the activity of man the maker, *homo faber*. Without him, there was no recognizable human world, just the endless process of nature, with every moment swallowed up and forgotten as soon as it had passed. Craftsmen produced the houses and domestic objects that gave character and continuity to human existence, an idea of survival beyond the birth and death of individuals; they created a recognizable human space for men to live in. Yet their products, too, were consumed and forgotten in the course of time; and their role in Greek life was not considered much higher than that of the slaves.

But the citizens, those men whose private needs were catered for by others in the privacy of their household, and who were otherwise free to go out and take part with their equals in the governance of the city or the people – these could, through their speech and their deeds in the sight of their fellow citizens, create an eternal memory for themselves. This was the sphere of 'action' in Arendt's meaning of the word; these were the members of the *polis* who were not bound by necessity, who knew the full scope of human freedom, its joys and its glory.

We can see from this account of the role of labour in human life why Arendt is sometimes so desperate about the twentieth century, where the obsession with labour and productivity seems often to have left men – as she puts it – with the distressing choice between productive slavery and unproductive freedom, and even the craftsman has largely vanished from the scene under the impact of mass production, the absorption of 'work' into 'labour'. She could have quoted William Wordsworth's cry 150 years earlier: 'Getting and spending we lay waste our powers.' (Yet with one of those imaginative leaps that again and again strike us in her work, Hannah Arendt can pause to give us a quite poetic glimpse of the real, if limited, happiness of the *animal laborans*, when she speaks of 'fruitful labour' as 'the human way to experience the sheer bliss of being alive which we share with all living creatures ... the only way men can remain and swing contentedly in nature's prescribed cycle, toiling and resting, labouring and consuming, with the same happy and purposeless regularity with which day and night and life and death follow each other.')

The heart of the book, however, is the lengthy consideration of 'action', where Arendt's picture of the free men of the Greek *polis* joining together in debate and deed leads her on to questions about the exercise of power. For her, true power is only found where men act freely together, consenting to decisions reached after free and impassioned argument between them. To be 'in power' means to be empowered by others. This, she believes, is the only kind of government that can ever endure; the only alternative is rule by force and violence, but this is always an inherently unstable form of government – and one which gives little joy to the tyrant who rules by such means. Arendt's vision of good government is essentially pluralistic, depending on the idea of many participants – ideally, in fact, all the people affected by the decisions reached; and her vision of a man's freedom equally requires the freedom of others, for without the freely given approval of others, there is no act worth performing – no human distinction and no good memory left behind.

She also observes that the poet and story-teller – a special kind of *homo faber* – are needed by those men who delight in 'action', for the full significance of a man's deeds can only be seen after his death, and only by those artists. Homer, for instance, told the tale of those 'free men' who participated in the Trojan war. Without tales being told of them, the glorious words and deeds of men would be as perishable as the simple metabolism of the life of the pure labourer.

Why was this vision of the 'human condition' so inspiring to many people? We can best approach that question by way of answer to various objections that have been made to Arendt's argument.

One persistent and powerful line of criticism has been that it shows, in its treatment of labour in both classical and modern times, 'an unfeeling disdain for the unpolitical masses' (the phrase comes from the American political scholar, Martin Jay), and an indifference to their welfare. Inequality and oppression have by no means vanished in the world today – even slavery still exists – but Arendt shows no interest in their abolition.

To this I think she would have replied that, in the Western world at least, the production of ample and even abundant material goods is fairly well assured by modern technology. It is precisely the enormous importance that is attached in practically all countries to economic and social improvement – the sphere of the Greek home or household – that needs to be questioned. She says in *The Human Condition* that no man can expect to live in the sphere of 'action' all the time; but she sees the opportunity to participate in this sphere as practically eliminated from most people's lives, as they go on from day to day as unprotesting job-holders, their existence regulated by a society almost solely interested in increasing its prosperity. She would, I think, have expected most people to have to work; equally, she had written bitterly of the unemployment in the pre-war years as one of the factors opening the way to Nazism; in practice, she was quite realistic and level-headed about the need for a job. But she thought that the overwhelming predominance of the 'social' or 'household' needs of man in the modern world had entailed a grievous loss to all men. It was not disdain that she felt for the 'unpolitical masses', but dismay at the thought of just what that phrase (her critic's own phrase, after all) expressed about their fate.

'But what about the right to vote in a representative democracy?' it might be asked. 'Does that not confer some genuine political freedom and power on all men who live under such a system?' The answer is that, of course, Hannah Arendt did not despise Western constitutional democracy – on the contrary, she was happy to live in a country governed under that system. But from her Weimar days, she had kept a profound suspicion of political parties; and even a healthy representative democracy – where political opinion was merely expressed through the vote – seemed to her a far cry from the assembling of all the free citizens to debate and decide in the Greek *polis*. She wanted to remind men of that.

However, another line of criticism often heard is that the idea of freedom extolled in *The Human Condition* is itself a very vague one. What matters did the ancient Greeks actually go to their assemblies to discuss? Arendt constantly avoids that question – and does not seem to care about the answer. The idea of their kind of freedom excites her – not any particular use to which it was put. She actually excludes many practical or administrative activities, like the application of the laws, from her exalted conception of political 'action'.

Again, how could we embody this kind of freedom – however much we might desire it – in our modern amalgam of democracy and bureaucracy? Even if we could, would that suffice to create the kind of world we wanted to live in? These, too, are questions to which Arendt scarcely begins to address herself in the book.

Perhaps the most interesting answers to them have been given by Jurgen Habermas, the professor of philosophy at Frankfurt University in recent years. A particularly remarkable fact is that Habermas is the leading figure in the 'second generation' of the Marxist Frankfurt School that we have already mentioned – a disciple of Adorno and Horkheimer. In his mixture of criticism and admiration for Hannah Arendt, we find a coming together of those two strands of thought that we saw, on the surface at least, as so strongly opposed to each other in the Germany of the 1920s and 1930s – the Marxist and the existentialist.

Habermas believes that Arendt's view of politics as implied in *The Human Condition* is unrealistic in the modern world, because it does not recognize the fact that the existing structure of society, with its maldistribution of freedom, can only be changed by some kind of forceful political strategy. He thinks it is impossible to exclude power struggles between organized groups – both those in power and those seeking power – from the proper domain of politics (nor, indeed, would Hannah Arendt have done so, when, in her *Totalitarianism* book, she described the relatively rational and respectable political world of the eighteenth century). Political parties, labour organizations and similar institutions seem to him to develop inevitably, and to be essential, in the conditions of modern politics. To suppose that society can be changed or even maintained just through public debate and agreement seems to him a totally vain hope.

Arendt meets these points to a small degree in *The Human Condition*. She acknowledges the importance of the law as an instrument for preserving stability and freedom. Otherwise, it is rather to individual attitudes of mind that she turns, as curbs on the misuse of political power.

One of these attitudes is forgiveness. Forgiveness, she thought, was a political matter, not just a personal one, because it enabled both the offenders and the offended to begin again, rather than 'confining them to a deed from which they could never recover'. Yet the idea of forgiveness needed as its counterpart the idea of punishment – another way of trying to bring an end to an offence and make a new beginning. In fact, she writes, 'men are unable to forgive what they cannot punish'; both these capacities of man, punishment and forgiveness, play their part in maintaining the order that is necessary for freedom.

The other attitude of mind that has this preserving power is the readiness to make promises. Promises, made mutually, are what keep a body of people together, acting in concert, and enable them 'to dispose of the future as though it were the present'. Hannah Arendt writes very beautifully and movingly about both these virtues – they are the only virtues, she says, that 'arise directly out of the will to live together with others in the mode of acting and speaking': they help us both 'to do and to undo', according to what our freedom requires.

But Habermas is surely right in thinking that such virtues,

however important it is to practice them, do not suffice to meet all the problems of the misuse or maldistribution of power in modern politics: they can only be the controlling virtues of a much more ideal world. Another political thinker and friend of Hannah's, Hans Morgenthau, observed that there was a romantic element in her conception of political freedom, and that certainly seems an apt comment here.

Yet Habermas also has a profound respect for Hannah Arendt's thought. He believes that her view of power as (in his own words) 'the ability to agree on a common course of action in unconstrained communication' is right, whether we are thinking of power as a means to achieve some practical goal, or whether we are thinking of it as an end in itself. In the first case, he argues, political parties or other bodies need that free, full agreement among their members simply in order to be effective. As for the second case, Habermas – as a post-war, new generation Marxist – believes that once men have achieved an acceptable degree of material equality, what is important for them is precisely to live in a world ordered by Hannah Arendt's notions of equal participation, defending the liberty of all against the threat of domination by any group or individual. In this 'intersubjective freedom' – to use a neo-Marxist, Frankfurt School bit of jargon – the dreams of the New Left seem to blend quite easily with Hannah Arendt's deeply conservative vision. That is why so many young people in the New Left seized on her works so eagerly in the late 1960s and 1970s. She seemed to offer guidance about the kind of 'participatory democracy' (as opposed to the comparatively impersonal 'representative democracy' of parties and voters) that they believed in.

Evidently, Arendt's tone is not the practical, pragmatic tone of normal, academic political science. It has a daring quality, constantly teasing out new and startling thoughts, shocking and challenging the reader. Another American political philosopher, Judith Shklar, has compared her with what Nietzsche called the 'monumental' writers of history, whose words are directed to the political actors themselves, reminding them of great deeds.

Yet Hannah Arendt also practised what Nietzsche called 'critical' history, the close and conscientious examination of a course of historical events, when it served her purpose; and one event took place while she was writing *The Human Condition* which she studied very carefully, since it seemed to her very much an example of the kind of 'action' that she dreamed of and demanded of men. This was the Hungarian uprising against the Russians in 1956. Later, she found a similar quality in the early stages of the American and French Revolutions in the eighteenth century: these form the subject of a book she published in 1965, *On Revolution*, and we shall consider her views on the Hungarian uprising along with that. More and more, we shall see, it was in revolutionary activity that she found hope, linking a high and ancient tradition of freedom with the aims of some modern revolutionary movements in her own original and provocative way.

More generally, we can say that *The Human Condition* is a profoundly heartening book to read. Where *The Origins of Totalitarianism* is like a manual of fear, *The Human Condition* is like a manual of hope. It is conceived primarily as a political work, a vision of what a world of free men might be like: that was the 'deliverance' it brought, to recall Sheldon Wolin's words. 'Her imperatives for political freedom enchant and reproach us,' said the poet Robert Lowell.

But it also speaks directly to the individual: it has an existentialist cutting edge, one might say, as well as a political cutting edge. It makes the reader stop again and again to consider whether he is allowing himself to be drawn into the aimless and evanescent process of labour and consumption; it encourages him, in powerful invocations, to be alert to his own constantly threatened freedom of 'action'. In the end, like *The Origins of Totalitarianism*, it is perhaps truest to see it as a resonant work of literature – a mighty echo of Homer and Thucydides for a world utterly different from theirs.

SIX

1958–61: American Questions

In 1958, the year of *The Human Condition*, Hannah was fifty-two. By now she was a commanding presence in her large circle of friends and colleagues. A younger friend, Jerome Kohn, has described her way of talking: 'Nuances of what she had said would recur to me for days afterwards . . . When I believed that I had understood several days later what she had said and would come back and say 'This is what you meant when we were talking about such and such", then it had always changed. This was a kind of intellectual frustration that was far from being negative – it made me think more and more. It was clear she was not simply recapitulating the thought of three days previous but she was thinking again. Whenever she spoke she thought – she thought on her feet, so to speak.'

Hannah thought hard, she had forceful opinions, and she could be very sharp-tongued. Another member of the *Partisan Review* set, Lionel Abel, reports a rebuke he received from her in that same year, 1958. Hannah, along with many other writers and scholars, had been invited to a meeting in a private house on East 87th Street to show support for Boris

Pasternak, who had been refused permission by the Soviet government to go to Sweden to receive his Nobel Prize. No one could agree what form of protest should be made. Hannah was insistent that any intervention they might make should be assured of helping Pasternak, not harming him. Abel had been drinking the host's bourbon steadily as the evening wore on, and suddenly suggested that the meeting should invite a Soviet literary journal to print Edmund Wilson's favourable review of *Dr Zhivago* from the *New Yorker*, in return for which they would try to get the *New Yorker* to print a Soviet critique of the novel. Hannah dismissed the suggestion airily. 'Schnapps' ideas,' she said – converting the liquor into her own European currency, as it were.

She joked and made tart epigrams like these: more often than not, her humour was of a satirical kind. A dry wit also runs through her writing, though less, perhaps, in *The Human Condition* than in her other books. Even there, however, in the middle of that moving section on promises that has already been quoted, we find a wry Jewish joke about 'Abraham, the man from Ur, whose whole story, as the Bible tells it, shows such a passionate drive toward making covenants that it is as though he departed from his country for no other reason than to try out the power of mutual promise in the wilderness of the world, until eventually God himself agreed to make a Covenant with him.'

The Blüchers often entertained after dinner, though Heinrich did not really like parties and had a habit of staying in his room when there were a lot of guests. If he decided to come out, he was quick to get into argument. Mary McCarthy's former husband, Bowden Broadwater, once described him as 'exploding like a little field-artillery piece' if someone said something that he found politically shocking.

Hannah would cook for her friends, but it was one of her slightly vain self-delusions that she could cook well. 'She could just about cook a potato,' a friend told me. An exception – an admired speciality of hers – was the Russian dessert *kissel*, a kind of cranberry jelly made with potato starch or corn starch.

She herself was, of course, often entertained, but she did not care for too much presumption on the part of her hosts. Once when a party was being laid on for her at a small college where she was a visiting lecturer, the head of the college inquired of an acquaintance of Hannah's what drinks she liked, and was told 'Campari soda'. It was not a drink frequently seen on American campuses at this time, but he made a point of getting some. When Hannah came in, however, he made the mistake of asking her 'Would you like a Campari soda?', gesturing in the direction of the tray where the Campari stood waiting. 'No, I'll have a bourbon,' she said firmly.

She had no regrets about being a woman: *'Vive la petite différence!'* was one of her mottoes. She gave her support to equal rights for women, but her view of the proper goal of the women's movement was very similar to the view she had always taken of the Jewish movement for equal rights in Europe before the war. She did not feel there was any need for women to abandon what had always been thought of as a feminine style of life, any more than there was any need for Jews to give up a Jewish way of life; these were private matters. Public campaigns should concentrate on establishing the legal acceptance of equality, until the state of affairs was reached where the participation of women in spheres that had been reserved for men simply went unremarked, with the women continuing to live in whatever style they wished. When she had taken up her teaching appointment at Princeton in 1953, she was annoyed when some of the male staff emphasized their pleasure that a woman was giving the Christian Gauss seminars for the first time. She felt herself being turned into an 'exception woman', like Rahel Varnhagen and the other 'exception Jews' who had been cosseted by German aristocratic society in the late eighteenth century; and she thought that to acquiesce in such treatment was a betrayal of other women. She simply wanted her sex to be taken for granted: 'I am not disturbed at all about being a woman professor,' she told an interviewer, 'because I am quite used to being a woman.'

Her friend Hans Jonas has given a vivid impression of her style in such matters. She discriminated unerringly, he says, between male and female friendships: 'I do not want to lose my privileges as a woman,' she would say, with a laugh. But she regarded men as far more prone to illusion than women. Sometimes when she was talking to Jonas and his wife, she would make a quick judgement on something, and he would ask her to justify it with some evidence. Hannah would exchange with Jonas's wife a glance of mutual understanding – comprising exasperation, compassion, even some tenderness – and say 'Ach, Hans!' Once he actually asked her, 'Hannah, please tell me, do you find me stupid?' 'But no!' – she was horrified – 'I only think you're a man.'

Not that her insistence on 'women's privileges' always

brought her friends, especially among other women. Daniel Bell has told me how if, for instance, she went with a husband and wife to the cinema, and they had to sit separated because the cinema was full, she would always carry the husband off to sit with her and leave the wife alone. There was more than one intellectual's wife in New York who greatly disliked her. Perhaps this manner of hers was also responsible for the loss of one of her dearest men friends, Randall Jarrell. Jarrell used to come often to read German poetry with Hannah, and in turn introduced her and Heinrich to the work of poets like Yeats and Emily Dickinson. She 'found his laughter right', she once said. But when he remarried, his new wife did not want him to go on seeing Hannah, and overnight he disappeared from her life. She wrote a fine essay about him after his death in 1965; she had never ceased to miss him.

Hannah was now beginning to think about her new book, in which she would follow up the ideas on 'action' and revolution that she had launched in *The Human Condition*. All her books lead on in this way from one to the other. But she was also getting more and more involved in American life, and in the two or three years immediately after finishing *The Human Condition*, she wrote some essays examining various practical questions in the light of her convictions. As usual, she was soon embroiled in controversy.

In 1957, troops tried to enforce the integrated education of black and white schoolchildren at Little Rock, the state capital of Arkansas, where the state governor himself was opposed to the new Federal laws. There were violent disturbances, and an angry debate raged across America.

In 1959 Hannah published an article in *Dissent* on the question, 'Reflections on Little Rock', that pleased practically nobody. Remembering her Jewish childhood, she was against any attempt by force – whether carried out by the government or by the blacks themselves – to integrate the black with the white community. In the first place, she thought such action deprived the blacks of their dignity: it put them in the role of the 'parvenus' that she had always thought so deplorable. And she was particularly upset by a photograph in *Life* magazine in which a small black girl, coming home under protection from her integrated school, was being howled at by a mob of white children. For her, this was just the sort of situation that children, above all, should not be exposed to; it was an assault on their pride and confidence in themselves that they might find it very hard to recover from. More generally, she thought such action by, or on behalf of, the black community concentrated on the wrong matters, from the point of view of their own interests. If people wanted to live in separate communities, then let them, she thought. What was far more important for a community suffering from disadvantages was to establish proper legal equality for its members, and to fight for that by political means. This was an exact echo of her views on the way in which discrimination against women should be combated. She thought that the laws against mixed marriages between blacks and whites, which in 1959 still existed in twenty-nine American states, were a much more appropriate target for all those who believed in equality in the United States. In other respects, she was sympathetic towards the rights of the different states to run their affairs in their own way: she saw the diversity of

Hannah aged 8 with her mother, Martha Arendt (later Beerwald)

Top left: Hannah's
father, Paul Arendt, just
before she was born
Top right: Hannah's
mother, Martha, at
home in Königsberg
Left: Hannah as a baby
with her grandfather,
Max Arendt

Top left: Hannah (left) dressed as a cigarette girl for a fancy-dress ball in 1922 when she was 16. With her is her stepsister, Eva Beerwald, dressed as the boy in the Swiss song who went begging with his marmoset
Top right: Hannah as a student on the balcony of the Königsberg house, Christmas 1928
Right: Hannah in Paris in the late 1930s

Martin Heidegger in
later life; as a younger
man he was Hannah's
professor and lover

Karl Jaspers, professor
and revered friend of
Hannah

Hannah in her thirties

Hannah with her first husband, Günther Stern (who later adopted the pen-name Anders) in about 1929

Hannah's second husband, Heinrich Blücher, as a young man

Hannah with Heinrich Blücher in about 1950

Hannah in Maine with one of her closest friends, Mary McCarthy

Hannah lecturing at Chicago University

Hannah teaching at the New School

Hannah in her early sixties

the different regions as one of the strengths of the Republic, a bulwark against the spread of mass, conformist man.

Hannah Arendt may not have judged very well the temper of any of the protagonists in the Little Rock battle – but that was not the kind of consideration that mattered to her. Her views were consistent with the long perspectives in man's history that she had tried to illuminate both in the *Totalitarianism* book and *The Human Condition*. Moreover, she changed her mind later on one point in the debate. The black writer Ralph Ellison argued, not angrily, that she had failed to understand how important for black children was the kind of baptism of fire, the painful initiation into the facts about their life, that they suffered in scenes like that shown in the *Life* photograph. It taught them courage. That argument touched a chord in Hannah; and she acknowledged in a letter to Ellison that the children might after all gain, rather than lose, from the experience.

Her thoughts remained with that little girl, however, and led her to reflect on more general questions of education, in an article called 'The Crisis in Education', published in *Partisan Review*. Children and young people loomed large in her mind at this time, partly because of her regular contact with students at different universities and colleges, and partly because she saw, both in the birth of children, and in the new freedom of action that each might display as it grew to maturity, the kind of 'beginning' with which her thought was now permeated – and which we saw anticipated in the last words of *The Origins of Totalitarianism*. She called her students 'the children', and she would sometimes murmur one of her favourite Goethe quotations, a line of *Faust*, about a bright student: 'For the soil again will grow them as it ever has before.'

'The Crisis in Education' is a very deeply felt and tender piece of writing. It argues that in the laudable attempt not to bully or impose ideas on children – an attempt born of the American belief in freedom – American education has gone to the other extreme and made it hard for them to grow up at all. Paradoxically, by giving them more freedom as children, it has diminished their freedom later, as adults. Wanting maximum freedom for them from the start, it has confined them to 'a world of children', from which adults are practically excluded, and when they are present claim no authority, not even the simple authority of knowing more than the children do. (In fact, they often do not know much more.) A child thus barred from the world of adults has little opportunity to rebel or 'do anything on his own hook'; on the contrary, he is more likely to be tyrannized by the majority of the other children – and end up as a conformist, if not a delinquent.

Children, she declares, need to be protected against the world in order to develop – but they must be steadily and thoroughly introduced to the realm created and inhabited by adults, for which they will themselves one day have to assume responsibility. And since that realm is old, 'always older than themselves', their learning will necessarily involve learning about the past. 'The function of the school is to teach children what the world is like', because only if they have that knowledge will they find the freedom to remake it. That vision of Hannah Arendt's with which we are by now becoming well acquainted shines through the concluding words of the article, in which she sums up its argument: 'Education is where we decide whether we love our children enough not to expel them from our world and leave them to their own devices, nor to strike from their hands the chance of undertaking something new, something unforeseen by us, but to prepare them in advance for the task of renewing a common world.'

That ideal for men, of inheriting with full understanding the human world into which we are born, and working together to re-create it from generation to generation, also underlies an essay called 'The Crisis in Culture' which Hannah Arendt wrote soon after 'The Crisis in Education'. Here she sees a threat to man's full freedom from the dominance in the modern world of a 'culture' shaped to the demands of mass society. She begins the article obliquely, with a side-thrust at the misuse of art by bourgeois society, which was so often only interested in it for its snob value. But even that society, though it 'devaluated cultural things into social commodities', did not 'consume' them completely. 'Even in their most worn-out shapes these things remained things and retained a certain objective character; they disintegrated till they looked like a heap of rubble, but they did not disappear.' Mass society, however, simply wants to 'consume' – it is the old *animal laborans* – and its 'culture' has finally degenerated into mere entertainment. Entertainment products simply while away the time, the time 'left over after labour and sleep have received their due'. Their excellence is not measured by the criteria of art objects, namely 'their ability to withstand the life process and become permanent appurtenances of the world'; they are 'consumer goods, destined to be used up, just like any other consumer goods'.

Against this picture she sets what she sees as a true relationship with art and culture. She finds that, in fact, it has something in common with the 'action' of the free man in politics. *He* has to choose and decide on right courses of action, in a real, resistant, objective world, sometimes agreeing with his equals, sometimes not. Equally, a true relationship with art is a matter of discriminating and deciding, in concert with one's fellow men – choosing those objects of artistic creation which seem to embody lasting beauty and truth, objects that help to create and sustain a desirable human world.

This is where her argument comes closest to the argument about the purpose of education in the other article. And this article, too, closes with inspiring words: 'Humanism is the result of an attitude that knows how to take care and preserve and admire the things of the world ... We may remember what the Romans – the first people that took culture seriously the way we do – thought a cultivated person ought to be: one who knows how to choose his company among men, among things, among thoughts, in the present as well as in the past.'

SEVEN

1961–63: The Eichmann Trial

In 1958, the year in which *The Human Condition* was published, *Rahel Varnhagen* was also published at last – almost twenty years after it was completed. It appeared first in Great Britain, and a German edition followed in 1959 (it had to wait till 1974 before it was published in the United States). In 1961, the essays on education and culture came out with four other essays that Hannah had written for various journals, in a book called *Between Past and Future: Six Exercises in Political Thought*.

Hannah's preface to this volume of essays included a passage on the 'treasure' discovered by men of the French Resistance: this treasure was the fact that, in their fight against the Nazis, they were stripped of masks and found out who they really were – a true existentialist discovery; and that they began, too, in Hannah's words, 'to create that public space between themselves where freedom could appear', instead of being trapped in the 'weightless irrelevance' of a private life concerned with nothing but itself. Hannah found a remark about life in the French Resistance made by the French poet, René Char, which exactly and beautifully illustrated this last idea: 'At every meal that we eat together,' Char wrote, 'freedom is invited to sit down. The chair remains vacant, but the place is set.'

As usual, ideas found in one work of Hannah's link up with ideas found in other works she was writing at the time. This passage relates closely to the main theme of her book *On Revolution*, which was by now practically finished; and its reference to the French Resistance connects it with a new undertaking Hannah had suddenly conceived for herself, and speedily arranged. This was to write a report for the *New Yorker* on the trial of Adolf Eichmann, due to begin in April 1961.

Eichmann had been a Gestapo officer in the Head Office for Reich Security under Himmler. He was not a high-ranking officer – he never got higher than lieutenant-colonel – but he had responsibility for Jews in the section dealing with opponents of the state. This meant, in practice, that he had organized the mass deportations and 'evacuations' of Jews that, after war broke out, took them straight to the killing camps. Jewish secret service men had kidnapped him in May 1960 in Buenos Aires and had flown him back to Israel, where he was to be tried for crimes against the Jewish people, crimes against humanity, and war crimes.

Hannah had not been at the Nuremberg trials of Nazi war criminals, and she felt that to attend Eichmann's trial and set eyes on him for herself was both an unexpected opportunity, and also something of an obligation on her, considering how much she had written about Nazism. The decision to go and write about Eichmann plunged her into the deepest controversy of her life, one that lost her many friends and made her many enemies. How far she anticipated this when she set out for Israel is hard to know: had she done so, one can be sure that it would still not have held her back.

From the start, she was scornful of the motives of the Israeli Prime Minister, David Ben-Gurion, in kidnapping Eichmann and staging the trial. From Ben-Gurion's pre-trial pronouncements, and from the opening words of the prosecutor, Gideon Hausner, it was clear to her that the trial was meant to be a demonstration to the world of both how much the Jews had suffered in history, and how determined Israel was to let the world know that they would not let it happen again. Ben-Gurion had practically said as much, when he declared that the trial would teach young Jews 'the most tragic facts in our history, the most tragic facts in world history', and that 'the Jews are not sheep to be slaughtered but a people who can hit back'.

Hannah did not at all like the tone of this approach to a trial – neither its rhetoric of self-pity and aggressiveness, both of which Hannah had criticized in the past as undignified and inappropriate attitudes for Jews; nor its suggestion that the outcome of the trial was a foregone conclusion (even if it was). But in due course she was to feel great respect for the judges themselves, who strictly concerned themselves with the point at issue: what Eichmann had actually done.

When she came to write her account of the trial, she did not dispute Eichmann's responsibility for the death of innumerable Jews, nor did she doubt that he should be hanged for his crimes, though her ideas about the legitimacy of the court and the justification for the death penalty were considerably more complicated than any expressed in the courtroom. It was on two points that were really incidental to the legal issue that her interest centred; and these were the two points with which she caused such deep offence.

The really remarkable feature of her five articles in the *New Yorker*, and the book based on them called *Eichmann in Jerusalem*, was its portrait of Eichmann the man. Hannah was astounded when she saw him and heard him speak. The press, and the prosecutor, had represented him as a pathological Jew-hater, a vicious sadist, a monster of depravity. She was rapidly persuaded by seeing him that he was none of these things. In a way, what he was – considering what he had done – was far more terrible: he was a feeble-spirited clown.

He was not insane: he was perfectly well aware that he had dispatched vast numbers of Jews to their death. But he had lost all power to distinguish between good and evil. He was still palpably proud that he had been such a faithful servant of Hitler and the other Nazi leaders. 'From a humdrum life without significance and consequence the wind had blown him into History, as he understood it, namely, into a Movement that always kept moving and in which somebody like him could start from scratch and still make a career.' He still regarded Hitler's edicts as unquestionable law, could still feel annoyed with colleagues who had put difficulties in his way when he was trying to organize his 'evacuations' and 'emigrations': he was still capable of burying beneath such euphemisms or clichés any sense of the enormity of what he had done. They were clichés that the Nazi leaders had provided for him, and he had properly and gratefully accepted them. Any moral unease that had in fact stirred in him at the thought of the killings, he had learned to accept as a discomfort he must put up with – one of the sacrifices it was necessary to make if one was to be a loyal servant of Hitler. As for anti-Semitism, he had never had any hostile feeling towards Jews; if anything, he had liked those he had known well. The fact that it was Jews that it was his duty to 'deport' was an irrelevance to him, a matter for his superiors. He had simply never found it necessary to think about these matters. And he was still so easily cheered up and comforted by clichés that he could say, just before he was hanged – after making a formal declaration that as a non-Christian Nazi he did not believe in the after-life – 'After a short while, gentlemen, we shall all meet again. Such is the fate of all men. Long live Germany, long live Argentina, long live Austria. I shall not forget them.' 'Under the gallows,' Hannah Arendt comments, 'his memory played him the last trick; he was "elated" and he forgot that this was his own funeral.'

This was the phenomenon that, in her most famous phrase, Hannah Arendt called 'the banality of evil' (it became part of the subtitle of the book, 'A Report on the Banality of Evil'). One can readily understand that the idea seemed bitterly offensive to many Jews: it could so easily be taken to diminish the significance of their sufferings. But Hannah Arendt was, I think, frequently and seriously misunderstood on this point. To say that Eichmann was not a monster was not to say that Nazi genocide was less than monstrous. Hannah Arendt's whole life's work shows how intensely she felt the monstrosity of Nazism. But she wanted to face the historical truth about it, and she wanted both the Jewish people and the rest of the world to face that truth, and to understand it;

for understanding, she was sure, was the first step in prevent-ing anything similar from ever happening again. Her interest had turned from the 'radical evil' that she had described as lying at the heart of totalitarianism, to this banal evil which was its essential instrument – an evil of which Eichmann was only one representative among the thousands, even millions, of Nazis and their acquiescent German followers. That was a kind of evil against which mankind might guard itself through self-awareness – in the knowledge that it was a kind of evil that any people might succumb to, if they were not vigilant enough.

One point, in fact, that Arendt especially stressed in her report was that 'the most potent factor in the soothing of Eichmann's conscience was that he could see no one, no one at all, who was actually against the Final Solution'. This led her directly on to the other argument that was to earn her so much disapproval, and even hatred. For it was not only among Germans, she said, that Eichmann could witness no resistance: it was also among the Jews, the victims, themselves that he met acquiescence and acceptance.

Here Hannah Arendt may have stepped, indeed, too indeli-cately. She described the way in which, in both Germany and the occupied countries, the locally recognized Jewish leaders were often given power by the Germans to help them in organizing the deportations; and Jewish officials did indeed co-operate with the Germans in many ways. Their motives were often of the highest: they believed, for instance, that Jewish policemen marshalling the deportees on to the trains would be 'more gentle and helpful' and would 'make the ordeal easier'. But Hannah Arendt condemned these actions in very strong terms: 'To a Jew,' she wrote, 'this role of the Jewish leaders in the destruction of their own people is undoubtedly the darkest chapter of the whole dark story.'

However, her evidence, in some of the cases she quoted, was not sufficiently authenticated. Nor did she show any awareness of the love in which many of the Jewish leaders, alive or dead, were held by those who had survived. This devotion was particularly strong in the case of the Jewish leader in Germany, Leo Baeck, whom she did not hesitate to describe as 'the Jewish *Führer*' (though she removed this description from later editions of the book). Above all, many readers felt that her condemnation showed no real understanding of the position in which Jews found themselves during the later stages of Nazi rule – and no sympathy towards them in the dreadful moral dilemmas they often had to resolve or the agonizing decisions they had to take.

She would not have defended any inaccuracies in her book, though she felt that most of her critics were far more indifferent to fact than she was. But her main defence of what she had written was along the same lines as her defence of her portrait of Eichmann. She was writing the truth about a collapse of the human spirit in order to praise and encourage its triumphs. She did not underestimate the difficulty of resistance to the Nazis – few of her critics seemed to have noticed a passage in the first chapter of her book, in which she quoted a question frequently asked in court, 'Why did you not revolt?', and commented: 'The court received no answer to this cruel and silly question, but one could easily have found an answer had he permitted his imagination to dwell for a few minutes on the fate of those Dutch Jews who in 1941 dared to attack a German security police department. Four hundred Jews were arrested in reprisal and they were literally tortured to death ... For months on end they died a thousand deaths, and every single one of them would have envied his brethren in Auschwitz. There exist many things considerably worse than death, and the S.S. saw to it that none of them was ever very far from their victims' minds and imaginations ...' Even so, she went on to praise many instances of resistance, including the uprising in the Warsaw ghetto and, above all, the concerted measures of the Danes, under occupation, to prevent harm coming to the Jews in Denmark, by holding the Germans off and using the Danish fishing fleet to ferry the majority of the Jews to Sweden. In Denmark, even the German authorities drew back from their task, and Arendt wrote, with a detectable air of rejoicing: 'The Nazis met with *open* native resistance, and the result seems to have been that those exposed to it changed their minds ... They had met resistance based on principle, and their "toughness" had melted like butter in the sun; they had even been able to show a few timid beginnings of genuine courage.' It was the point she wanted to make. Otherwise, the history of acquiescence and co-operation 'offers the most striking insight into the totality of the moral collapse the Nazis caused in respectable European society – not only in Germany but in almost all countries, not only among the persecutors but among the victims'.

While she was in Jerusalem covering the trial, Hannah saw a lot of her old friend, Kurt Blumenfeld, who introduced her to many leading Israelis. On her way back she stayed in Zurich with Karl and Gertrud Jaspers; and Heinrich came to

Zurich to join her. It was his first visit to Europe since he and Hannah had escaped in 1941, and his first meeting with Jaspers. The two men liked each other immediately, and Hannah was delighted and relieved. She and Heinrich went on for a tour of Italy, where Heinrich met an old song-writing friend from Berlin days, Robert Gilbert. Hannah cheerfully described this summer of 1961 as an 'orgy of friendship'.

Back in America again, she finished her book *On Revolution*, and set to work on her Eichmann report. But two alarming events were in store. In October, Heinrich was taken to hospital with a ruptured blood-vessel in his brain. Luckily he had recovered, without any after-effects, by the end of the year. Then in March 1962, a taxi Hannah was taking in New York was hit by a lorry, and she was badly hurt in the head. For two months she could not work; afterwards, she went round wearing a veil, then an eye-patch – looking, according to one friend, like a pirate.

The *New Yorker* articles appeared in February and March 1963; and the storm broke immediately. Several Jewish organizations put out statements fiercely criticizing Hannah; Israeli lawyers and politicians publicly condemned her. She had expected this; what she had not realized was that so many members of her New York circle would turn against her. Robert Lowell has described the reaction: 'No society is more acute and over-acute at self-criticism than that of the New York Jews. When Hannah's *Eichmann* was published, a meeting was summoned by Irving Howe and Lionel Abel, normally urbane and liberal minds. The meeting was like a trial, the stoning of an outcast member of the family. Any sneering over-emphasis on Hannah, who had been invited but was away teaching in Chicago, was greeted with derisive clapping or savage sighs of amazement ... Alfred Kazin walked self-consciously to the stage and stammered, "After all, Hannah didn't kill any Jews." He walked off the stage laughed at as irrelevant and absurd.'

Many friends stood by her, both Jews and non-Jews – Mary McCarthy, Hans Morgenthau, Daniel Bell, Bruno Bettelheim, Dwight Macdonald; and Karl Jaspers, far away in Switzerland. But there was a long breach in her friendship with Hans Jonas, to whom she had been so close ever since Freiburg days – a breach healed eventually by Jonas's wife. Hannah was especially hurt – and indignant – that *Partisan Review* chose to publish a hostile review of the book, written by Lionel Abel. Worst of all for her was the news that Kurt Blumenfeld had died in Israel in a state of outrage with her. He had been too ill to read the articles himself, and had depended on reports given to him by other people. Hannah was sure that if he had been able to judge for himself, he would not have felt as he apparently did at the last.

However, another meeting was very different. In July, Hannah herself spoke to the Jewish students at Columbia, on the invitation of the Jewish counsellor at the university, Albert Friedlander. There was an enormous crowd in the large hall; outside, people were sitting on the fire-escapes, and beating at the windows to be allowed in; newspaper men and Israeli consular officials were insisting on their right to be present.

Hannah was in her element at this meeting, glowing with excitement. She spoke for an hour, then answered questions for an hour. People jumped up and accused her of making

common cause with the Nazis, but she was absolutely un-
moved; she precisely and coldly demonstrated how they were
wrong. Some people had come not so much because they
were hostile as because they had been plunged into anxiety
by what she had written; a good half of the audience were
young students who were entirely on her side. Calm and
cogent, she slowly pacified the waves of emotion that had
been running through the hall, and at the end her friends
formed a phalanx round her to escort her out. At the meeting
she had been imperious in manner, but afterwards she was
relaxed and full of good humour. Perhaps for a moment she
had felt something of what her ancient Greek heroes had felt,
when they spoke in the *polis*.

The last important exchange over her Eichmann book that
Hannah herself took part in was in the pages of *Encounter* in
January 1964. An old, dear friend, the Jewish religious
scholar, Gershom Scholem, had written to her grieving that
she showed no love for the Jewish people. This letter was
published in *Encounter* along with Hannah Arendt's reply to
it. Scholem had observed that she was 'one of the intellectuals
who came from the German Left', and she correctly denied
that, saying that 'If I can be said to "have come from
anywhere", it is from the tradition of German philosophy' –
a remark that was itself, not surprisingly, used against her as
the controversy went on. What in fact she wanted to stress
was that she had come into politics not as a left-wing intellectual but as a Jew; and she insisted now on her unquestioning
Jewishness. 'To a Jew . . .', she had prefaced her words, when
she had described the actions of the Jewish councils under
the Nazis as 'the darkest chapter' of the story. Her answer to

Scholem's charge was that for her it was not merely a matter of 'loving' or 'believing in' the Jews, but that 'I belong to them as a matter of course, beyond dispute or argument'. It was exactly the same attitude as her mother's had been, when Hannah was a little girl in Königsberg, learning how to face anti-Semitic remarks at school. That total belonging was her justification for all she had written about the Holocaust. As for Israel, in particular, she loved it – in Mary McCarthy's words – as a mother. The novelist remembers Hannah murmuring the words 'I'm so worried about Israel' over and over again, early one morning, as they drove along together in a taxi. That kind of love explained why the failings of the Jews were a graver matter to her than the failings of all other peoples.

A last set of reflections by Hannah Arendt on the Eichmann case appears in a talk that she broadcast on BBC radio (and which was reprinted in the *Listener*) later in 1964. This talk was entitled 'Personal Responsibility Under Dictatorship'. Moving away from the particular events that took place in Nazi Germany, it sketched out some more general moral and philosophical conclusions she had come to. She emphasized a point that she had touched on in *Eichmann in Jerusalem*: that what had enabled some people to resist co-operation with the Nazis was a particular way of thinking and judging that they had. They did not see morality as simply obedience to rules and laws – that easily led a man into obeying evil 'laws' in a dictatorship. 'Their criterion,' she wrote, 'was a different one; they asked themselves to what extent they would still be able to live in peace with themselves after having committed certain deeds; and they decided that it would be better to do nothing, not because the world would then be changed for the better, but because only on this condition could they go on living with themselves. Hence, they also chose to die when they were forced to participate. To put it crudely, they refused to murder, not so much because they held fast to the command "Thou shalt not kill", as because they were unwilling to live together with a murderer – themselves.'

She concluded that this kind of thinking and judging – 'the habit of living together explicitly with oneself, of being engaged in a silent dialogue between me and myself' – was not only the basis for any trustworthy morality, but was actually 'at the root of all philosophical thinking'. Ideas like this were to lead Hannah Arendt ultimately to return, in the final years of her life, to the pure philosophical thinking of her younger days.

EIGHT

1963–70: A True Revolution

By now the Blüchers had moved into their third and last home in New York, an apartment at the top of a tall house in Riverside Drive on the Lower Hudson. It was a quieter neighbourhood, and the apartment had wide, spectacular views over the river – a place suited to a philosopher, as Helen Wolff said. In the entrance-hall, a blow-up photograph of Kafka faced the visitor. Robert Lowell often used to visit Hannah there in the late afternoon, to eat nuts and hear her talking with 'merry ease': 'the conversation rambled through history, politics and philosophy, but soon refreshed itself on gossip'. But that ease inside the flat was always preceded, for Lowell, by a feeling of apprehension on first seeing the apartment house: it gave him 'the thrill, the hesitation and helplessness of entering a foreign country, a north German harbour, the tenements of Kafka. Its drabness and respectability that hid her true character also emphasized her unfashionable independence.'

Hannah, as she approached the age of sixty, had found a new calm in herself. It was partly a result simply of seeing at close quarters, in the dock at Jerusalem, the face of evil –

Eichmann's face – and finding it such a poor thing. The world seemed no less terrible, but it seemed less demonic after that. When she had had her accident in the taxi, she had also discovered an unexpected calm in her spirit. In a letter to Mary McCarthy, she described how she came to in the car on her way to hospital: 'I tried out my limbs, saw that I was not paralysed and could see with both eyes; then tried out my memory – very carefully, decade by decade, poetry, Greek and German and English; then telephone numbers. Everything all right. The point was that for a fleeting moment I had the feeling that it was up to me whether I wanted to live or die. And though I did not think that death was terrible, I also thought that life was quite beautiful and that I rather like it.'

In 1965, when the spiritual diaries of Pope John XXIII were published, she wrote a review of them in the *New York Review of Books*, in which she spoke admiringly of his simplicity of spirit and peacefulness of mind. The simple basic chord to which his mind was tuned, she wrote, was the ability to say without any reservation, mental or emotional, 'Thy will be done'; and she quoted what she considered his greatest words, which he spoke when he was dying. They are very reminiscent of her own words to Mary McCarthy after the accident: 'Every day is a good day to be born, every day is a good day to die.' Without having any Christian belief, she acknowledged here a debt to Christianity, which we can also find in her early studies of St Augustine, in the surprising passage on the importance of forgiveness in the very worldly pages of *The Human Condition*, and in many passing remarks she made to friends in the course of her life – like one that Frederick Morgan remembers her making at a holiday reading-party arranged by Mary McCarthy at her house in Maine: 'If Jesus Christ wasn't the son of God, then he ought to have been!' Her political vision, with its overriding theme of the joy of speaking and doing in the public world, has nothing to do with Christian tradition; but a vision of Christian 'unworldliness' always haunted the corners of her mind, and played its part in her private life.

However, she was far from finished with politics; nor was she abandoning a life of action. She took more holidays than she had done when she was younger, in a country hotel that she and Heinrich liked at Palenville on the edge of the Catskill mountains north of New York, or in Switzerland; but her public life was more vigorous than ever. She was constantly giving lectures or attending seminars – or, nowadays, collecting honorary degrees. When she stopped in London to see her stepsister, Eva would go and visit her in her hotel, feeling that Hannah was the busier woman; Hannah stayed twice at large hotels in London, but was miserable in them because there was no table for her typewriter, and afterwards she always stayed at a small hotel which provided her with a table she could work at. She was always very cheerful when Eva and she sat recalling episodes from their German days; and when Eva once mentioned the Eichmann affair she dismissed the matter breezily, saying *'Ach, der Eichmann Rümmel'* – 'Oh, that Eichmann fuss'. She was well off now, and very generous, supporting Israeli charities – especially during the 1967 war – and providing money to help with the education of many young people, the children of her surviving relatives and of old friends. When Eva succeeded with a claim she made for compensation for the loss of the old Königsberg house, Hannah insisted that Eva should take the whole sum, though part of it was due to Hannah.

Hannah's book *On Revolution* had come out in 1963, a few months after the Eichmann book and inevitably somewhat overshadowed by it. But it was a very important book for her. In the Hungarian uprising – or revolution, as she preferred to call it – in 1956, she had seen an event which embodied so many of her hopes for men. It was an uprising against totalitarianism – the first really widespread and dramatic revolt against Stalinism – and it answered exactly to her wishes for what might have happened under the Nazis. It answered, too, to the vision of *The Human Condition*: a whole people was making a new beginning, 'acting' together in speech and deed. And the specific form the uprising took – the immediate formation throughout Hungary of workers' and revolutionary councils – was precisely what she saw as the ideal alternative to government through political parties: such councils had been found in the 1848 revolutions, in the Paris Commune in 1871, and even in the first days of the October Revolution in Russia in 1917.

The uprising was defeated, but its flames, she wrote, 'illuminated the immense landscape of post-war totalitarianism for twelve long days. This was a true event whose stature will not depend on victory or defeat; its greatness is secure in the tragedy it enacted.' It was the kind of 'spontaneous revolution' that her mother's heroine, Rosa Luxemburg, had believed in, something which conservatives and liberals, radicals and revolutionists had all denied the possibility of, as being nothing more than a noble dream. And until it was suppressed by the Russians, it had worked: there was no chaos, no crime, no fanaticism, just twelve days of true fraternity and true democracy. All these thoughts she had put down soon afterwards, in an epilogue to the second edition of *The Origins of Totalitarianism*, which was published in 1958.

Now, in her book on revolution, she identified two more great moments in modern history that came near to embodying her vision. The first was the French Revolution, which began by seeking to create a constitution that would ensure liberty for the French people, but which ended, in her view, with the Rights of Man that had at first inspired the revolutionaries being swallowed up by the Rights of the Sans-Culottes – the 'Trouserless'. The early leaders of the revolution, the Girondists, were above all concerned with the proper form of the new constitution. But Robespierre and the Jacobins cared more about 'liberating the suffering masses' than 'emancipating the people', and the Constitution of 1791 remained a piece of paper, its authority shattered by the violent tide of events before it was even formally adopted.

Hannah Arendt saw the Reign of Terror and the disappearance of liberty as a direct consequence of the French Revolution turning away from what she thought was the only goal a revolution could hope to achieve – the creation of new power by men making decisions together in freedom and equality – to a preoccupation with 'the social question', the material needs of the masses. That, as we have noted already, was not for her the proper concern of politics – especially revolutionary politics, which was perhaps the only true form of politics open to modern men.

But – like a beautiful present from Fate, one might think –

Hannah Arendt found something close to her idea of a true revolution in her country of adoption: in the American Revolution, a generation before the French. What particularly impressed her about the new America, after it had declared its independence and risen against the rule of the British, was the way in which there had been 'a spontaneous outbreak of constitution-making in all thirteen colonies', while the Founding Fathers sought to create an American Constitution in which freedom for all men should be preserved not just by edict of the law, but precisely by the separation and balancing of powers.

She acknowledged that the American Revolution took place under much happier circumstances than the French: there was no pressing 'social question', inasmuch as America knew nothing of the predicament of mass poverty, and the people already had widespread experience of self-government – they were not rebelling against an absolute power like that of the French kings. Nevertheless, she writes with delight and enthusiasm of the spirit in which the American Republic was founded: the revolution 'was made by men in common deliberation and on the strength of mutual pledges'.

She felt that the Revolution had not fulfilled all the promises held out by its beginnings; and she especially regretted, as the Founding Father Thomas Jefferson himself had done, that the town-meetings, 'the original springs of all political activity in the country' and the equivalent of the revolutionary councils elsewhere, were not incorporated into the Constitution. Yet she believed that in many respects the United States was still close to the spirit of the Founding Fathers; perhaps she still remembered that woman in whose house she had lived when she first arrived in America. *On Revolution*, like all her books, had its critics, who attacked it for misleading historical analysis or for a lack of political realism; but it answered many of the questions put to her about the modern application of the ideas she had expounded in *The Human Condition*.

In the middle and late Sixties, most of Hannah's writing appeared in magazines, especially the *New Yorker* and the *New York Review of Books*; and in 1968 she brought out a volume of her essays about people, *Men in Dark Times*. It is one of the richest and most easily enjoyable of her books. It includes the essays or lectures already mentioned here on Pope John XXIII, Jaspers, Walter Benjamin, Waldemar Gurian and Randall Jarrell; the other figures discussed are the philosopher Lessing, Rosa Luxemburg, the Danish story-teller Isak Dinesen, Hermann Broch and Bertolt Brecht.

In her preface, she described what she meant by 'dark times': these were times when public figures conceal the truth about what is happening in the world behind noble-sounding obfuscation and double-talk. She quoted Heidegger's epigram on such times, 'The light of the public obscures everything' – she still warmed to all that was fine in Heidegger. And she hoped that the men and women she had written about had kindled at least a weak, flickering light to shed some illumination over 'the time span that was given them on earth'.

But, as usual, there was something in the book to excite hostility in both political camps. This time it was her essay on Brecht, which had first been published in the *New Yorker*. She profoundly admired some aspects of Brecht, and thought him a true poet – 'someone who must say the unsayable, who must not remain silent on occasions when all are silent'. But she thought that his very compassion for the oppressed had led him into evil – an echo, here, of her reflections on the French Revolution – for it had induced him to lie in praise of Stalin and Stalinism. However, she defended a remark Brecht had made about the victims of Stalin's show-trials to the American anti-Stalinist writer, Sidney Hook: 'The more innocent they are, the more they deserve to die.' She believed that 'tricky' Bert Brecht had meant that the guilt of those innocent victims lay in their *failure* to oppose Stalin, and she claimed that this was one of Brecht's veiled criticisms of Stalin. Hook was outraged by this interpretation, being convinced that Brecht's remark was wholly cynical, putting the needs of the Communist Party, however cruel and unjust the consequences, above all other considerations. Hannah rejoined that Brecht had just been too clever for Hook.

At the same time, though, Hannah fiercely criticized Brecht for some odes to Stalin that she claimed he had written. The English Brecht scholar, John Willett, denied that Brecht had ever written such poems, and Hannah was unable to produce them; but she firmly maintained that she was right and that they existed.

Hannah had been deeply shocked and upset by the assassination of President Kennedy in 1963, and she knew that many Americans felt that their own country was moving into 'dark times'. But she continued to have faith in the Republic during the Sixties, and did not immediately oppose the American intervention in Vietnam, though she came out against it when it began to turn into full-scale war.

In 1966, one of the first student sit-ins took place in Chicago, where she was lecturing at the time. The students were protesting – in many cases, against their own interest – at the selective call-up for Vietnam of the academically less successful students, and Hannah was greatly impressed by this moral rebellion. She went to see some students in the building they had occupied, and had a long talk with them – admiring their spirit, but telling them that what they were doing was nevertheless illegal, and adding as a parting shot that if they were going to stay they should at least keep the place clean! She was also exhilarated at first by the student rebellion in France and America in 1968 – Daniel Cohn-Bendit, or 'Red Dani', one of the French student leaders, was the son of old friends from her years in Paris – but she did not approve when, at Columbia, the revolt changed from an attack on government defence research being carried out by the university, to an attack on the academic freedom of the university itself, with threats of it being taken over by 'the people'.

These events, and various public discussions in New York that she took part in, turned Hannah's thoughts to the question of the use of violence in revolt and revolution; and in 1970 she published a short book, *On Violence*, the most taut and elegant book she wrote. She was sympathetic by now to the principle of civil disobedience, and even considered that a right to non-violent civil disobedience might be introduced as an amendment into the American Constitution. But in the book she argued persuasively that the use of violence in times of rebellion is always in the end self-defeating.

She drew up in fresh terms her by now familiar contrast

between violence and power. True and lasting power, she continued to believe, only manifested itself when men acted in concert. She quoted a remark by C. Wright Mills, 'The ultimate kind of power is violence', only to disagree with it completely. Her point was that when there was no longer agreement between men who had originally set out to fight a common foe – and when commands were therefore no longer obeyed – the means of violence were useless. 'Everything depends on the power behind the violence', power in her sense of the word; otherwise there is simply aimlessness and chaos. And if violence succeeded temporarily, as of course often happened, it always had to yield to some kind of collective power in the end for the revolution to continue. Its only alternative was to follow violence with more violence, or terror, endlessly. Her conclusion was that 'the danger of violence, even within a non-extremist framework of short-term goals, will always be that the means overwhelm the end ... Violence, like all action, changes the world, but the most probable change is to a more violent world.'

Therefore she was using all her eloquence and powers of argument to discourage American dissidents from turning to violence. She particularly deplored the change she could see taking place in the New Left, from a belief in non-violence to a belief that violence was necessary. To her, they were in danger of turning dream into nightmare.

Before she had finished *On Violence*, Hannah had lost her mentor for so many years, that man of peace, Karl Jaspers. He died, aged 86, in February 1969. Hannah went to Basle for the funeral and for a memorial service, where she spoke of the need to continue in our minds our conversation with the dead ones we have loved. In October of the following year, quite suddenly, Heinrich died of a heart attack, collapsing on a sofa at home. While Hannah had gone out and lived her public life largely on her own, Heinrich had continued teaching quietly at Bard College; he had never written anything. His great achievement had no doubt been all he had given Hannah, in wisdom and in confidence in herself. She felt alone and empty, and went on wearing black, for a long time after he died.

But a few weeks after his death, she received a strange proposal of marriage – from the dishevelled W. H. Auden, whose life was famous for its disorganization. I think that Isaiah Berlin was right when he said to me that this was actually insulting to Hannah – it was like trying to turn her into a German *Hausfrau*. And of course the idea was an impossible one for her. But she felt a great pity for him, and tried to show her regret and her appreciation of him. She spent much energy trying to persuade him how sensible it would be to have two suits, so that he could get one of them cleaned – but her efforts were unsuccessful, and he continued to wear the only suit he had. He died three years after Heinrich; and Hannah wrote a tender obituary of him in the *New Yorker*.

NINE

1971–75: Last Inquiries

Hannah stayed on in the Riverside Drive apartment after Heinrich's death, because there she could feel his absence more acutely, and remember him best. Her friends had become more important to her than ever, especially Mary McCarthy and her husband Jim West, with whom Hannah spent long holidays in America and Europe and with whom she was now constantly in correspondence. And she was still making new friends: the young German writer, Uwe Johnson, who was visiting America, became a close friend at this time, and wrote after her death of the gift she had for speaking with complete truthfulness to friends. David Green, who taught with her in Chicago, said that by now her lined face reminded him of a Rembrandt portrait, and Uwe Johnson tells another story about her striking appearance. She once took him walking round a mainly Jewish part of New York, and she read out for him, from the faces of the passers-by, the details of where in Europe they had come from, what they did, what their standing was. She wondered if her face could be read in the same way. Johnson said to her, 'Oh Hannah! Hannah!

You have a face like seven synagogues!' – and she laughed at his joke and his frankness.

At sixty-five, her energy and curiosity seemed as great as they had ever been. The student of hers who was later to become her biographer, Elisabeth Young-Bruehl, described on BBC radio how she was Hannah's 'tour guide' on a visit to London Hannah made in 1971. Hannah wanted to go to all kinds of buildings that had round council rooms in them, including the baronial council room that is attached to Wells Cathedral in the West of England. She wanted to see the architectural embodiment of the kind of debating democracy she believed in, which she thought was particularly strong in the British tradition of government. And, as we shall see, in America she was engaged in political controversy practically to the day of her death.

But in the last five years of her life, her thinking, for the most part, turned away from political ideas and the claims of the *vita activa* to the classic preoccupations of the *vita contemplativa*: the kind of questions with which she had begun her philosophical career as a student at Freiburg. She said to her old friend of those days, Hans Jonas, 'I have done my bit in politics, no more of that; from now on, and for what is left, I will deal with transpolitical things.' She was going to 'get down to philosophy' – and she added a German slang phrase, *'Jetzt geht's um die Wurst'*, 'It's the moment of truth' or, more literally, 'Now it all comes down to the sausage.'

She planned a work that would do for the life of contemplation what *The Human Condition* had done for man's active life in the world. Like that book, it would be divided into three parts: 'Thinking', 'Willing' and 'Judging'. In fact, only the first two parts were written, and they appeared as a book after her death with the title *The Life of the Mind*.

Hannah approached this topic in her own idiosyncratic way. She took no account of the modern English and American philosophers who had considered, with stringent logical analysis of their propositions, the 'philosophy of mind'. On the other side of the coin, she showed no interest in Freud and his picture of human nature. But she ransacked medieval theologians and the great figures of German philosophy for illustrations congenial to her way of thinking. *The Life of the Mind* has to be seen as a source of interesting and suggestive ideas, rather than as a fully worked-out philosophical statement according to the rigorous analytical requirements of contemporary Anglo-Saxon philosophy.

She seems to have been pulled in two directions in this work. On the one hand – following Kant, her philosophical predecessor in Königsberg – she wanted to assert that true thinking was not just a matter of the intellectual discovery of more or less reliable truths, in the fashion of science; it was a larger, more meditative brooding on the nature of things, not practical or obviously useful, yet with the power sometimes to bring the whole being of man nearer to wisdom or virtue. At the same time as she asserted this argument, she was expressing hostility to those traditional philosophers – they included Heidegger, in his later writings – who thought that philosophy had nothing to do with politics and the active life, but drew its adherents into wholly unworldly contemplation. These arguments she set against a rich historical background of philosophical ideas; but the issues remain imprecise and unresolved in the book.

Some readers have found the most valuable parts those in which the connection is clear with ideas in her earlier work. For instance, she continued to reflect in *The Life of the Mind* on the point she made about Eichmann: that 'thinking', the soundless dialogue one carries on with oneself, may in times of emergency be the way to independence of judgement and moral courage, with real political effects:

'When everybody is swept away unthinkingly by what everybody else does and believes in, those who think are drawn out of hiding because their refusal to join is conspicuous and thereby becomes a kind of action.'

More generally, *The Life of the Mind* is imbued with a feeling which, in Hannah Arendt's own life, went right back to the influence of Heidegger – a feeling of awe and amazement at Being-in-the-world, and an attitude (in Sheldon Wolin's words) 'of wonder and affection toward the diversities that appear in everyday life'. It leads to the idea that a proper expression of true thinking is found in poetry and story-telling. This whole aspect of the book is ruled over by the remark of Cato's that Hannah Arendt had put at the end of *The Human Condition*, as a reminder there of the other realm, the realm of the contemplative life, which that book had avoided dealing with: 'Never is a man more active than when he does nothing, never is he less alone than when he is by himself.'

But *The Life of the Mind* also echoes *The Human Condition* in one way: everywhere we find the implication that, just as in the *polis* men came together and revealed themselves to each other in debate and deeds in the realm of action, so in the realm of thought it is proper for them to join together in common contemplation of the universe. The world of thought is not one of secrets, but is open to the minds of all men. And that kind of coming together is proper to man, unlike the practice of pure introspection or meditation on one's private moods, for which Hannah Arendt felt contempt to the end.

Hannah was already working on *The Life of the Mind*, when she was invited to give the Gifford Lectures at Aberdeen University in the spring of 1973. She prepared the 'Thinking' section of the book for that occasion; and when she was asked to give a second series the following year, she got the 'Willing' section ready. But she did not complete that series; at the end of the first lecture she had a heart attack.

She made a good recovery in the summer of 1974, and Mary McCarthy helped her with the final form of these two sections of the book. Later, after Hannah's death, Mary McCarthy devotedly worked over them again to prepare them for publication. Hannah had for a long time now been writing in English, but always had some help with the final 'Englishing'; and Mary McCarthy's account of working with her, printed as a postface to *The Life of the Mind*, is a vivid one, telling how Hannah chafed at the mysterious constraints of English, often writing long Germanic sentences that had to be 'unwound or broken up ... She tried to get too much in at once; the mixture of hurry and generosity was very characteristic.' But the outcome in all her later books was a very pungent and distinctive style. Robert Lowell thought that she was absolutely right to write in English. He felt that her finest sentences were 'a wrenching, then a marriage of English and German', and that if she had written in German and let someone else translate her, 'her freshness, nerve and actuality would have suffered a glaze, a stealing of her life'.

Hannah had been invited to go back to Aberdeen in 1976 to complete her unfinished series of lectures, and she went on rewriting the 'Willing' portion, very concerned now with focusing on what were for her the strengths and weaknesses of Heidegger's varying views on the subject. Late in the summer of 1974 she decided she must visit him; but it was an unsatisfactory meeting, with Heidegger's wife insisting on being present while they talked. In 1975 she went again, only to be struck by how old and deaf he had become even within the year: in fact, he was to die in May 1976, less than six months after Hannah. She told Mary McCarthy that old age was not a matter of growing weaker oneself, but of experiencing a kind of deforestation around one, as familiar faces steadily disappeared. She turned for comfort to Cicero's treatise on old age, *De Senectute*, characteristically deciding that nothing sensible had been written about growing old since he wrote it.

But she was still not quite finished with politics. In 1971, she had written an article in the *New York Review of Books* called 'Lying in Politics'. This was a review of *The Pentagon Papers*, a forty-seven-volume record from official papers of American decision-making policy in Vietnam. The book revealed a long history of public deception and government self-deception, showing propagandists and experts working together to manipulate knowledge of what was happening in Vietnam, for the sake of the public image of the American government, and also for the government's own self-satisfaction. To this story Hannah brought her memories of collective myth-making in Nazi Germany; and she wrote fiercely and bitterly about such things, with their strong taint of totalitarianism, happening in the United States. The only comfort she could find was that Robert McNamara, the Secretary of Defence, had himself commissioned the study, in an attempt to find out what had gone wrong in Vietnam; that one of its authors had leaked it to the press; and that the *New York Times* had published long extracts from it, although at the time it was classified as 'Top Secret'. That had led, finally, to its full publication – something, she thought, that could hardly have happened anywhere except in the USA. The article was included in what was to be the last book by her published in her lifetime, *Crises of the Republic*, which came out in 1972: besides 'Lying in Politics', it included a revised version of her short book, *On Violence*, her reflections on civil disobedience and some further remarks on revolution.

In the next two or three years, Hannah, like many others, came to feel that 'dark times' had really descended on America. The Vietnam war had escalated, and dragged Cambodia into the circle of destruction; finally, in 1973, there had been a scrambled withdrawal of American troops, leaving America's allies in South Vietnam to their fate. Meanwhile, the Watergate affair had exploded: President Nixon had been accused of organizing criminal operations against his political opponents, and had resigned from the Presidency in 1974.

The last year of Hannah's life was a hectic one. In April 1975, she went to Denmark to receive the Sonning Prize for Contributions to European Civilization. In May she made her strongest attack yet on what she had been watching happening in the United States: she had been invited to speak at an American Bicentennial celebration in Boston, and she used the occasion to give a talk called 'Home to Roost', in which she declared that the USA might be standing 'at one of those decisive turning points of history which separate whole eras from each other'. What she especially wanted to say was like a sequel to what she had written in 'Lying in Politics': that it was essential for America not to fall into a new phase of myth-making about Vietnam, and now about the Watergate affair. Again, she saw the threat of totalitarianism looming up.

The speech was published in the *New York Review of Books* and was widely discussed – but besides the many enthusiasts, there were also many vigorous critics of it. In September, just before Hannah's sixty-ninth birthday, there was a sharp attack on her in *Commentary* by Nathan Glazer, in an article called 'Hannah Arendt's America'.

Glazer began with the simple, heartfelt sentence, 'Hannah Arendt is our teacher'; and he went on to praise *The Origins of Totalitarianism* and *The Human Condition*. But he argued that Hannah Arendt's latest attack on America was superficial, and that, for all its mistakes, the USA had consistently stood up for freedom and democracy, both at home and abroad, in a way she might have been expected to approve of. Many of the recent strains in American life, he argued, had come precisely through the extension of liberty: the creation of new rights for black people, for students, for criminals, for the unemployed. And he believed that through the best of the mass media, and the liberal majority in Congress, the nation was kept well-informed of the facts, and was thoroughly discouraged from taking refuge in myths.

However, Hannah had left New York again and was spending the summer in Switzerland, at the Casa Barbete in the Alps at Tegna, where she and Heinrich had stayed in the last summer of his life. On the way, she had carried out her last duty to Karl Jaspers, sorting out his letters for a month at the German Literature Archive at Marbach, as one of his executors. It was after that that she had paid her visit to the aged Heidegger. Now, in Switzerland, she was living quietly, reading 'good old Kant', still working on *The Life of the Mind*, with friends coming and going. Elisabeth Young-Bruehl conveys something of her serenity of mind in an incident from this summer that she described in a reminiscent article in *Social Research*. A neighbour's cat had lost her kittens, and mourned for them for three days, then resumed its normal habits. Hannah told her visitors about the cat as dinner was being prepared; and she ended with a quotation from the *Iliad*, which she first spoke in Greek – the words of Achilles to the mourning Priam:

> 'Now let us think of supper,
> For even fair-haired Niobe thought of eating,
> She whose twelve children died in her halls,
> Her six daughters and her six vibrant sons.'

In Hannah's words, Elisabeth Young-Bruehl says, there was 'a strange, profound simplicity that did justice at once to her own life, Priam's and the cat's.'

She returned to Riverside Drive in October, and held a big birthday party. After that she stayed mainly at home, not much inclined to go out, in a neighbourhood that had seen

133

a big increase in muggings. She had two guests to dinner on 4 December, and as she was sitting down, about to pour the coffee for them, she fell back. She had had another heart attack, and she died soon afterwards, without becoming conscious again. In her typewriter was the first page of the last section of *The Life of the Mind*: all it had on it was the title, 'Judging'.

Her funeral service, like Heinrich's, was held in the Riverside Memorial Chapel, and it took a similar form to his, part secular, part Jewish. *Kaddish*, the Jewish funeral prayer, was said for her. Mary McCarthy thought that in her coffin, in the funeral parlour, 'with the lids veiling the fathomless eyes, that noble forehead topped by a sort of pompadour, she was not Hannah any more but a composed death-mask of an eighteenth-century philosopher'. Hans Jonas spoke to the 300 mourners, recalling her as a friend. Trying to sum up her life's work, he said: 'She set a style of inquiry and debate which will ensure that no cheap formula for the human predicament will pass muster, as long as her example is remembered.'

Books by Hannah Arendt

The Origins of Totalitarianism, Harcourt, Brace, New York, 1951. Published in Great Britain under the title *The Burden of Our Time*, Secker and Warburg, London, 1951. The second, enlarged, edition, containing a new epilogue about the Hungarian uprising, was published in both countries under the title *The Origins of Totalitarianism*, Meridian Books, New York, 1958; Allen and Unwin, London, 1958.

The Human Condition, Chicago University Press, Chicago and London, 1958.

Rahel Varnhagen, East and West Library, London, 1958; Harcourt, Brace Jovanovich, New York, 1974.

Between Past and Future, Viking Press, New York, 1961; Faber and Faber, London, 1961.

Eichmann in Jerusalem, Viking Press, New York, 1963; Faber and Faber, London, 1963.

On Revolution, Viking Press, New York, 1963; Faber and Faber, London, 1963.

Men in Dark Times, Harcourt, Brace, New York, 1968; Cape, London, 1970.

On Violence, Harcourt, Brace, New York, 1970; Allen Lane, London, 1970.

Crises of the Republic, Harcourt Brace Jovanovich, New York, 1972; Penguin Books, London, 1973.

The Life of the Mind, Two volumes. Harcourt Brace Jovanovich, New York, 1978; Secker and Warburg, London, 1978.

Books about Hannah Arendt

Margaret Canovan, *The Political Thought of Hannah Arendt*, Harcourt Brace Jovanovich, New York, 1974; Methuen, London, 1977.

Bhikhu Parekh, *Hannah Arendt and the Search for a New Political Philosophy*, Humanities Press, Atlantic Highlands, 1981; Macmillan, London, 1981.

Elisabeth Young-Bruehl, *Hannah Arendt: For Love of the World*, Yale University Press, New Haven and London, 1982.

George Kateb, *Hannah Arendt: Politics, Conscience, Evil*, Rowman and Allanheld, Totowa, New Jersey, 1983; Martin Robertson, Oxford, 1984.

INDEX

Abel, Lionel, 91–2,109–10
Adorno, Theodor, 30–32, 45, 86
Arendt, Hannah (Johanna),
  articles:
      'The Crisis in Education (*Partisan Review*), 97–9
      'Lying in Politics' (*New York Review of Books* 1971), 130–31
      'Organized Guilt and Individual Responsibility' (*Jewish Frontier* 1945), 60
      'Reflections on Little Rock' (*Dissent* 1959), 96
      'What is *Existenz* Philosophy?' (*Partisan Review* 1946), 21–2, 76
  books:
      Between Past and Future: Six Exercises in Political Thought (1961), 101–2
      Crises of the Republic (1972), 131
      Eichmann in Jerusalem (1963), 102–13
      The Human Condition (1958), 25, 29, 73, 78–92, 101, 115, 117, 126,`128
      The Life of the Mind (1978), 126–30, 133, 134
      Men in Dark Times (1968), 43, 120–21
      Origins of Totalitarianism (1951), 15, 40–2, 52–3, 59–72, 77–8, 89–90, 118
      Rahel Varnhagen: The Life of a Jewish Woman (1958), 32–6, 48, 101
      On Revolution (1963), 89, 102, 109, 117–20
      On Violence (1970), 122–3
  other writings:
      'The Crisis in Culture' 99–100
      'Home to Roost' (1975), 132
      Die Liebesbegriff bei Augustin (The Concept of Love in Augustine) (doctoral thesis 1929), 29
      'Personal Responsibility Under Dictatorship', 112
      Die Schatten ('The Shadows'), 24
Arendt, Martha *see* Beerwald
Arendt, Max, 14
Arendt, Paul, 13–14
Aron, Raymond, 44

MORE ABOUT PENGUINS, PELICANS, PEREGRINES AND PUFFINS

For further information about books available from Penguins please write to Dept EP, Penguin Books Ltd, Harmondsworth, Middlesex UB7 0DA.

In the U.S.A.: For a complete list of books available from Penguins in the United States write to Dept DG, Penguin Books, 299 Murray Hill Parkway, East Rutherford, New Jersey 07073.

In Canada: For a complete list of books available from Penguins in Canada write to Penguin Books Canada Ltd, 2801 John Street, Markham, Ontario L3R 1B4.

In Australia: For a complete list of books available from Penguins in Australia write to the Marketing Department, Penguin Books Australia Ltd, P.O. Box 257, Ringwood, Victoria 3134.

In New Zealand: For a complete list of books available from Penguins in New Zealand write to the Marketing Department, Penguin Books (N.Z.) Ltd, Private Bag, Takapuna, Auckland 9.

In India: For a complete list of books available from Penguins in India write to Penguin Overseas Ltd, 706 Eros Apartments, 56 Nehru Place, New Delhi 110019.

A CHOICE OF PENGUINS

A CHOICE OF PENGUINS

☐ *Man and the Natural World* **Keith Thomas** £4.95

Changing attitudes in England, 1500–1800. 'An encyclopedic study of man's relationship to animals and plants . . . a book to read again and again' – Paul Theroux, *Sunday Times* Books of the Year

☐ *Jean Rhys: Letters 1931–66*
 Edited by Francis Wyndham and Diana Melly £4.95

'Eloquent and invaluable . . . her life emerges, and with it a portrait of an unexpectedly indomitable figure' – Marina Warner in the *Sunday Times*

☐ *The French Revolution* **Christopher Hibbert** £4.95

'One of the best accounts of the Revolution that I know . . . Mr Hibbert is outstanding' – J. H. Plumb in the *Sunday Telegraph*

☐ *Isak Dinesen* **Judith Thurman** £4.95

The acclaimed life of Karen Blixen, 'beautiful bride, disappointed wife, radiant lover, bereft and widowed woman, writer, sibyl, Scheherazade, child of Lucifer, Baroness; always a unique human being . . . an assiduously researched and finely narrated biography' – *Books & Bookmen*

☐ *The Amateur Naturalist*
 Gerald Durrell with Lee Durrell £4.95

'Delight . . . on every page . . . packed with authoritative writing, learning without pomposity . . . it represents a real bargain' – *The Times Educational Supplement.* 'What treats are in store for the average British household' – *Daily Express*

☐ *When the Wind Blows* **Raymond Briggs** £2.95

'A visual parable against nuclear war: all the more chilling for being in the form of a strip cartoon' – *Sunday Times*. 'The most eloquent anti-Bomb statement you are likely to read' – *Daily Mail*

CLASSICS IN TRANSLATION
IN PENGUINS

☐ *Remembrance of Things Past* **Marcel Proust**

☐ Volume One: *Swann's Way, Within a Budding Grove*   £7.95
☐ Volume Two: *The Guermantes Way, Cities of the Plain*   £7.95
☐ Volume Three: *The Captive, The Fugitive, Time Regained*   £7.95

Terence Kilmartin's acclaimed revised version of C. K. Scott Moncrieff's original translation, published in paperback for the first time.

☐ *The Canterbury Tales* **Geoffrey Chaucer**   £2.95

'Every age is a Canterbury Pilgrimage . . . nor can a child be born who is not one of these characters of Chaucer' – William Blake

☐ *Gargantua & Pantagruel* **Rabelais**   £3.95

The fantastic adventures of two giants through which Rabelais (1495–1553) caricatured his life and times in a masterpiece of exuberance and glorious exaggeration.

☐ *The Brothers Karamazov* **Fyodor Dostoevsky**   £4.95

A detective story on many levels, profoundly involving the question of the existence of God, Dostoevsky's great drama of parricide and fraternal jealousy triumphantly fulfilled his aim: 'to find the man in man . . . [to] depict all the depths of the human soul.'

☐ *Fables of Aesop*   £1.95

This translation recovers all the old magic of fables in which, too often, the fox steps forward as the cynical hero and a lamb is an ass to lie down with a lion.

☐ *The Three Theban Plays* **Sophocles**   £2.95

A new translation, by Robert Fagles, of *Antigone, Oedipus the King* and *Oedipus at Colonus*, plays all based on the legend of the royal house of Thebes.